Praise for *Cold in July*

"It's a major novel, full of darkness, humor, passion, and truth."
—Lewis Shiner, author of *Glimpses* and *Mozart in Mirrorshades* (with Bruce Sterling)

"I can't think of a more remarkable suspense novel in the last few years. *Cold in July* has it all...."
—Ed Gorman, author of *The Poker Club*

"*Cold in July* is more than a novel of detection; it is an odyssey into the dark recesses of the human psyche...."
—Loren D. Estleman, author of *Burning Midnight*

Praise for Joe R. Lansdale

"A folklorist's eye for telling detail and a front-porch raconteur's sense of pace."
—*New York Times Book Review*

"A terrifically gifted storyteller."
—*Washington Post Book Review*

"Like gold standard writers Elmore Leonard and the late Donald Westlake, Joe R. Lansdale is one of the more versatile writers in America."
—*Los Angeles Times*

"A zest for storytelling and gimlet eye for detail."
—*Entertainment Weekly*

"Lansdale is an immense talent."
—*Booklist*

COLD IN JULY
JOE R. LANSDALE

Cover photo © 2014 by BSM Studio
Cover and interior design by Elizabeth Story

Tachyon Publications
1459 18th Street #139
San Francisco, CA 94107
(415) 285-5615
tachyon@tachyonpublications.com

smart science fiction & fantasy
www.tachyonpublications.com

Series Editor: Jacob Weisman
Project Editor: Jill Roberts

ISBN 13: 978-1-61696-161-9

Printed in the United States of America by Worzalla

First Tachyon Edition: 2014
9 8 7 6 5 4 3 2 1

ALSO BY JOE R. LANSDALE

Hap and Leonard mysteries

Savage Season (1990)
Mucho Mojo (1994)
The Two-Bear Mambo (1995)
Bad Chili (1997)
Rumble Tumble (1998)
Veil's Visit: A Taste of Hap and Leonard (1999)
Captains Outrageous (2001)
Vanilla Ride (2009)
Hyenas (2011)
Devil Red (2011)

The "Drive-In" series

The Drive-In: A "B" Movie with Blood and Popcorn,
Made in Texas (1988)
The Drive-In 2: Not Just One of Them Sequels (1989)
The Drive-In: A Double-Feature Omnibus (1997)
The Drive-In: The Bus Tour (2005)
The Complete Drive-In (2009, omnibus)

The "Ned the Seal" trilogy

Zeppelins West (2001)
Flaming London (2005)
Flaming Zeppelins: The Adventures of Ned the Seal (2010)

Other novels

Act of Love (1981)

COLD
IN JULY

JOE R. LANSDALE

TACHYON
SAN FRANCISCO

I'd like to thank Gary L. Brittain, David G. Porter, and Bob LaBorde for their advice on certain technical matters in this novel.

INTRODUCTION
JIM MICKLE

There's a little saying that "it takes an average of seven years to get a movie made." It's not a popular saying but one that was often repeated to me over the (coincidentally) seven years it took to get *Cold in July* made into a film. It usually was said just before recounting the legend of how *Forrest Gump* sat around for a decade before it was finally made. Now that I think of it, maybe it's just something the producers made up to make me feel better as time ticked away and Joe Lansdale's novel sat bound in its own pages, never making it anywhere near a silver screen.

I had first read it at the end of 2006. We had just put the finishing touches on *Mulberry Street*, our first feature film, and were starting to line up film festivals where it would be introduced to the world. *Mulberry Street* was sort of an urban riff on zombie films—in this case, rat zombies taking over lower Manhattan—told through the eyes of the screenwriter and lead actor, Nick Damici, who lived (in the movie and in real life) in an old-school New York neighborhood fighting off the encroaching yuppies and eminent domain that threatened to change the neighborhood.

I grew up in rural Pennsylvania, and now having worked on the script, the shoot, and the editing intensely for about two years in hot, cramped, overstuffed New York City, I was kind of done with city tales. I hadn't thought about anything but Nick fighting rat zombies in the back alleys of Lower Manhattan for as long as I could remember. I went to bed thinking/worrying about it, usually dreamed/nightmared about it, and thought of it first thing when I woke up. I needed something to cleanse the palate creatively, and the best way I knew to escape the city was to read Joe Lansdale.

My sister and I were raised on Bruce Campbell. We probably watched *Army of Darkness* once a day for a solid year while growing up. That movie is a big part of why both of us are in the film business now. One night, driving back into the city after a break from college, we drove past the Angelika Film Center and saw on the marquee a *Bubba Ho-Tep* Midnight Show with none other than Bruce Campbell in attendance. We pulled over, crapped our pants, bought tickets, and got to see Ash in person, all while being introduced to the wild world of Lansdale.

After that night, I'd always make it a point to read Joe's work. He somehow manages to capture all the little things I love about B movies and pulpy stories, but he gives them all heart, and he knows small-town life better than anyone. His stories are unpredictable but naturally so, and he's never afraid to throw a bunch of different genres into the blender to see what comes out. I had a connection to his writing that I didn't really have to other authors, and so after the sound mix to *Mulberry Street*, I picked up a dog-eared copy of *Cold in July* and hopped onto a subway home.

"That night, Ann heard the noise first." That first line did its job, yanking me right out of underground New York City and straight into Joe's world. It was like putting on noise-canceling headphones for your brain. By the time I got to my subway stop, I had met Ben Russel. I walked home and kept reading, entered my apartment, and told myself that I would just read another chapter or two before making dinner. I sat down on my bed and didn't move or eat for the rest of the night. Sometime after midnight, Jim Bob

Luke said, *"It's Howdy Doody time,"* and my hands started sweating to the point that I had to wipe them off on my jacket (which I still hadn't taken off).

By the time I reached the last word, my blood ran ice cold, my brain was all twisted up, and I couldn't really move. The only thing I could think to do was turn the book over and start reading again from the first line, wondering how the hell Joe had managed to start from that scene and make it to that ending. It was film noir, western, samurai, morality tale, and even horror all mixed together in one spicy stew. It felt familiar but completely new at the same time, like when you hear a great song for the first time. It did everything modern screenplays never seemed to do for me. My mind had indeed taken a vacation from urban horror and rat zombies, and in one night it had found a new obsession.

Immediately, I gave the book to Nick Damici and my producer (and girlfriend) Linda Moran. Their response was the same as mine. I'm pretty sure Nick sat down and started adapting it just a few days later, rights or no rights. Coincidentally, *Mulberry Street* was to have its U.S. premiere at the South by Southwest Film Festival in Austin, Texas, just a few weeks later, where Joe was scheduled to hold a book signing. He was kind enough to hear our plea to adapt the book, and he watched our little rat-zombie movie and even appeared to like it. Joe had optioned movie rights for about a million things over his career and by this point had even optioned *Cold* previously for a number of years, but, like a lot of his stuff, it was a little too dark or a little too complex for someone to ultimately green light. We told ourselves we could crack it.

Nick's first pass of the script was somehow even longer than the novel. Like true fanboys, we held on to every word, every character, and somehow managed to take a relatively short, fast-paced book and adapt it into a loooooong, bloated screenplay. Over the years we managed to pare it down and get to the essence of what we loved, learning the art of adaptation as we went while Linda helped us keep the script lean and mean like the book itself.

I'd guess that Nick has written more than a hundred drafts of the script. Every year or so, Joe would read a new draft and chime in with his thoughts to tell us when we'd strayed too far from the fence.

Lots of financiers and producers liked the project immediately. "The guy who wrote *Bubba Ho-Tep* and the guys who made that little rat-zombie movie? And the cover's got a dude with a gun on it? Tell me more!" But for the better part of six years, we could never get over the hump. Financiers came and went. Actors attached themselves and then left to do TV series and never came back. Money people said it was too dark, too violent, too fast, too slow, too character driven, too genre, not believable, not crazy enough, too Texan, even too American.

All the while, we plowed ahead. Linda and I spent a weekend in Nacogdoches, Joe's hometown, soaking in the flavor of East Texas and dreaming up a shoot that wouldn't actually happen for another four years. During the wait, Nick was even hired to write *another* Lansdale adaptation from Joe's short story "The Pit."

Twice, we wound up making other movies—*Stake Land* and *We Are What We Are*—and each time I'd have to send that sad little e-mail to Joe that said we were not giving up on *Cold* but were going to spend the next year and a half doing another film, and that our hope was that this film would finally help get *Cold* made. Finally, after *We Are What We Are* played Sundance and Cannes, making for happy investors and happy critics, and after we had made three successful independent films, the chips fell into place.

The green light came with a random meeting with the amazing Michael C. Hall at a party and a Southwestern breakfast with Sam Shepard in Santa Fe, topped off with the news that Don Johnson wanted to play Jim Bob. Joe even came to the shoot for about two weeks, bringing his wonderful family along, watching as a story he dreamed up some twenty-four years ago was playing out for real, right down to that first bullet hole in the wall.

COLD IN JULY

As I write this, I'm in the same position I was with *Mulberry Street*, about to enter the sound mix and filled with excitement and fear over the fact that we're premiering in one month at the 2014 Sundance Film Festival, where Joe will get to watch as Vinessa Shaw snaps awake, hearing that first sound. By the time you read this, you'll know whether the film went over well and what kind of release it will get, and you'll probably see trailers of Don Johnson saying, "It's Howdy Doody time" before he cocks his shotgun.

Until then, I dare you to read this book and not fall deeply in love the way we all did seven years ago.

Jim Mickle
December 2013

Whoever fights monsters, should see to it that in the process he does not become a monster.

—Nietzsche

PART ONE
SONS

1.

That night, Ann heard the noise first.

I was asleep. I hadn't slept well in a while due to some problems at work, and the fact that our four-year-old son, Jordan, had been sick the previous two nights, coughing, vomiting, getting us up at all hours. But tonight he was sleeping soundly and I was out cold.

I came awake with Ann's elbow in my rib and her whisper, "Did you hear that?"

I hadn't, but the tone of her voice assured me she had certainly heard something, and it wasn't just a night bird calling or a dog working the trash cans out back; Ann wasn't the frighty type, and she had incredible hearing, perhaps to compensate for her bad eyesight.

Rolling onto my back, I listened. A moment later I heard a noise. It was the glass door at the back of the house leading into the living room; it was cautiously being slid back. Most likely, what Ann had heard originally was the lock being jimmied. I thought about Jordan asleep in the room across the hall and gooseflesh rolled across me in a cold tide that ebbed at the top of my skull.

I put my lips to Ann's ear and whispered, "Shhhh." Easing out of bed, I grabbed my robe off the bedpost and slipped it on out of habit. Our night-light in the backyard was slicing through a split in the curtains, and I could see well enough to go over to the closet, open the door and pull a shoe box down from the top shelf. I put the shoe box on the bed and opened it. Inside was a .38 snub-nose and a box of shells. I loaded the gun quickly by feel. When I was finished, I felt light-headed and realized I had been holding my breath.

Since Jordan had been sick, we had gotten in the habit of leaving our bedroom door open so we could hear him should he call out in the night. That made it easy for me to step into the hallway holding the .38 against my leg. In that moment, I wished we lived back in town, instead of here off the lake road on our five-acre plot. We weren't exactly isolated, but in a situation like this, we might as well have been. Our nearest neighbor was a quarter mile away and our house was surrounded by thick pine forest and squatty brush that captured shadows.

It was strange, but stepping into the hall, I was very much aware of the walls of the house, how narrow the hallway really was. Even the ceiling seemed low and suffocating, and I could feel the nap of the carpet between my toes, and it seemed sharp as needles. I wondered absently if it were deep enough to hide in.

I could see the flashlight beam playing across the living room, flitting here and there like a moth trying to escape from a jar, and I could hear shoes sliding gently across the carpet.

I tried to swallow the grapefruit in my throat as I inched forward and stepped gingerly around the corner into the living room.

The burglar's back was to me. The night-light in the backyard shone through the glass door and framed the man. He was tall and thin, wearing dark clothes and a dark wool cap. He was shining his light at a painting on the wall, probably deciding if it was worth stealing or not.

It wasn't. It was a cheapo landscape from the county fair. Ann and I knew the artist and that was the reason we bought it. It covered that part of the wall as well as a Picasso.

The burglar came to the same conclusion about its worth, or lack of, because he turned from the painting, and as he did, his light fell on me.

For a moment we both stood like fence posts, then his light wavered and he reached to his belt with his free hand, and instinctively I knew he was reaching for a gun. But I couldn't move. It was as if concrete had been pumped into my veins and pores and had instantly hardened.

He brought the gun out of his belt and fired. The bullet snapped past my head and punched the wall behind me. Without really thinking about it, I jerked up the .38 and pulled the trigger.

His head whipped back, then forward. The wool cap nodded to one side but didn't come off. He stepped back stiffly and sat down on the couch as if very tired. His revolver fell to the floor, then the flashlight dropped from the other hand.

I didn't want to take my eyes off the man, but I found I was tracking the progress of the flashlight as if hypnotized by it. It whirled halfway across the floor toward me, stopped, rolled back a pace, quit moving, its beam pooled at my feet like watery honey.

Suddenly I realized my ears were ringing with the sound of gunfire, and that the concrete had gone out of me. I was shaking, still pointing the gun in the direction of the burglar, who seemed to be doing nothing more than lounging on the couch.

I took a deep breath and started forward.

"Is he dead?"

I damn near jumped a foot. It was Ann behind me.

"Goddamn," I said. "I don't know. Turn on the light."

"You okay?"

"Except for shitting myself, fine. Turn on the light."

Ann flicked the switch and I edged forward, holding the gun in front of me, half-expecting him to jump off the couch and grab me.

But he didn't move. He just sat there, looking very composed and very alive.

Except for his right eye. That spoiled the lifelike effect. The eye was gone. There was just a dark, wet hole where it used to be. Blood welled at the corners, spilled out, and ran down his cheek like scarlet tears.

I found myself staring at his good eye. It was still shiny, but going dull. It looked as soft and brown as a doe's.

I glanced away, only to find something equally awful. On the wall above the couch, partially splashed on the cheap landscape, I could see squirts of blood, brains and little white fragments that might have been bone splinters. I thought of what the exit wound at the back of the man's head would look like. I'd read somewhere that the bullet going out made a hole many times bigger than the one it made going in. I wondered in a lightning flash of insanity if I could stick my fist in there and stir it around.

It wasn't something I really wanted to know.

I put the revolver in the pocket of my robe, wavered. The room got hot, seemed to melt like wax and me with it. I went down and my hands went out. I grabbed at the dead man's knees so I wouldn't go to the floor; I could feel the fading warmth of his flesh through his pants.

"Don't look at him," Ann said.

"God, his goddamn brains are all over the fucking wall."

Then Ann became sick. She fell down beside me, her arm around my shoulders, and like monks before a shrine, we dipped our heads. But instead of prayers flying out of our mouths, it was vomit, splattering the carpet and the dead man's shoes.

Jordan slept through it all.

2.

The cops were nice. Real nice. There were ten of them. Six in uniform, the others plainclothes detectives. The detectives weren't anything like the television cops I expected. No frumpy guys in open trench coats dripping chili dogs down their ties. They even wore nice suits. No bad manners. Very polite. No suspicions. They took in what had happened easily and surely.

The man in charge of the investigation was a lieutenant named Price. He looked like a movie star. Must have been about thirty-five. Had perfectly combed hair and bright blue eyes that matched his expensive suit. He had such a shoe shine it jumped at you.

He came over and touched me on the arm. "You doing okay, Mr. Dane?"

"Yeah," I said, still tasting the aftereffects of the vomit. "Peachy."

"You couldn't have done much else. He shot at you first."

I nodded. I didn't regret what I had done, just hated that I had been forced to do it.

"I had to kill a man once," Price said. "In the line of duty. But it was tough getting over. To be honest, you never quite get over it. If you're human you shouldn't. But you can't blame yourself."

"I don't. But it doesn't make me feel any better."

Ann had gone into the bedroom with Jordan, who had finally awakened to the sounds of the police poking around. She was keeping him in the back so he wouldn't have to see the dead man.

Dead man.

I glanced at the couch where the man had been sitting, at what I imagined was the indentation his body had made, but knew truthfully was a permanent impression formed by long wear and weak springs. There was a messy swipe of blood on the cushions to mark his passing, and the stuff on the wall and across the landscape looked in that odd moment like a wild abstract painting.

I remembered how the justice of the peace had come in looking sleepy-eyed, wearing a pajama top and jeans with one pants leg stuck down in a cowboy boot, the other pulled over. He pronounced the man dead and grumbled about how even small towns should have coroners. He went away then, and the police checked the corpse over, took photographs, and two men from the funeral home carted off the body.

I looked at the wall some more, and the blood mess no longer looked like a painting, but like someone had tossed some rotten tomatoes against it. That thought made me woozy, and I dry heaved because there was nothing left inside me to throw up.

I took a deep breath, but that didn't help. It contained the sour aroma of stale vomit and the coppery smell of blood.

"Better sit down," Price said.

"I'm all right," I said.

"Sit down anyway."

I guess my face had gone white. Price helped me to a chair and squatted down beside me.

"Should I get you some water?" he asked. "Something?"

"I'm all right. Do you people know this man by any chance?"

"Quite well. Name is Freddy Russel. Small-time guy. Did burglaries from time to time, mostly in this area, which is where he's from, I'm sorry to say. Been in and out of the joint, just like his old man. You did the creep a favor."

"Sure."

"You'd be surprised. Sometimes guys like that get careless on purpose, just hoping to get caught, get back to the joint where it's easier for them. Or maybe they hope for something a little more permanent. Like a bullet."

"He wasn't trying to get killed when he took a shot at me."

Price smiled. "Good point. So much for backyard psychology."

"Thanks for trying to make me feel better. It's decent of you."

"Like I said, I been through this. Listen, you think you could come down to the station? Let me get a formal statement? Won't take long. Patrol car will take you and bring you back. We'll leave a patrolman here with your wife and boy. She can come in tomorrow sometime to make her statement."

"All right," I said. "Let me tell Ann and I'll get dressed."

3.

It was easy. I told Price the same thing I told him at home, except it was more detached now, as if it had happened to someone else and I had witnessed it from a distance.

The room where he took my statement smelled of stale cigarette smoke, but that was the only thing that fit my image of a police station. The room looked more like an insurance company office. I had seen too many damn television shows and movies, expected dust, cobwebs, empty coffee cups, half-eaten pizza and too much light.

There wasn't much in the room in the way of furniture or decoration. Some citations on the wall, a file cabinet, a neat desk, a typewriter, paper in the roller, and Price behind the keys. In fact, Price and I were the only ones in the room.

It took twenty minutes for me to tell it again, top to bottom.

"What now?" I asked.

"Not much," Price said. "It'll go to the grand jury. They'll look over your statement, your wife's, mine, then they'll No Bill you. You won't even have to go to court."

"You're sure?"

"Open-shut case of self-defense. He broke in with intent to rob, took a shot at you. Your gun was legal. He's a known crook, you're an upstanding citizen in the community. We haven't any reason to suspect you of anything. It's over. Except for your gun. We'll keep it a while, until you get the No Bill, then we'll return it. I'll have an officer take you home."

When I got home the policeman who had stayed with Ann nodded at me and went away with the other officer. I sank down in the living room chair and looked at the couch. I didn't think I could ever sit there again. I determined that tomorrow I would have it carried off and buy a new one. I wanted to get rid of that bloodied landscape too and have the wall repainted. Christ, I felt like moving, and would have if I could have afforded it.

Ann sat on the edge of the chair and put her arm around me. "You okay?"

"Okay as I get. Go to bed, honey. I'll come along."

"I'm going to clean up a little...before Jordan gets up."

It occurred to me what she meant, the wall, couch and painting. She just couldn't put it into words.

"Is it all right if we do?" I asked. "Evidence and all. Won't the police mind?"

"The officer told me any time we wanted to clean up to go ahead. They've taken photographs, done all they intend to do."

"I'll help."

We got a plastic bucket of warm, soapy water and rubbed the couch down, threw the painting away, and wiped the wall as clean as we could get it. The couch was ruined. The blood had soaked into it, turning it dark in spots, giving the room a faint odor to remind us of what had happened.

We cleaned up the carpet and put baking soda down to get rid of the smell of vomit, and it helped a little. When we were finished, I poured the soapy water into the kitchen sink, watched it swirl darkly down the drain, tossed away the rags we'd used and sprayed some air freshener about.

I don't know why, but the freshener struck me as funny in a grim kind of way. I kept imagining a commercial for air freshener where the announcer was saying how it covered up not only the odor of fish and onions, but blood, brains and vomit as well.

Ann showered and I washed up in the bathroom sink, feeling like Lady Macbeth struggling with her damn spot, even though there wasn't a drop of blood on me.

Death in reality certainly wasn't like television death. It was nasty and it smelled and it clung to you like a bad disease.

Self-defense or not, I didn't feel like Dirty Harry. I just felt bad, worse than I had ever felt in my life.

"Let's go to bed," Ann said. She was stepping out of the shower and she looked good. Thirty-five years had been kind to her. Her breasts sagged a little maybe, but the rest of her was nice and the breasts were nothing to run me off. She was my woman and I loved her, and I knew she was offering herself to me. I could tell by the way she moved as she pulled the shower cap off and let her long blond hair fall like a shower of light onto her shoulders, by the slightly exaggerated stretches and the way she slid the towel slowly up her long legs and moved it seductively over her damp pubic hair.

She smiled at me. "We can snuggle, you know?"

"I'm not really sleepy," I said stupidly.

"So, we can snuggle a lot. Sleep later."

"We can try that," I said. "Go ahead, and I'll be to bed in a moment. Got a few things to do yet."

She finished drying, stepped into her panties, extending her legs through them nicely. It was almost enough to excite me, even after what had happened earlier. Almost.

She put on her robe, kissed me on the cheek and went out of there with her soft soap scent lingering in the air.

I took a leak, showered, and brushed my teeth. I put on my robe, went through the house testing locks on the doors leading outside. They were all fine except for the jimmied door, of course. I checked the windows too, and when I was finished in Jordan's room, I stopped by his bed and put his teddy bear back under the covers and tucked them around him. I felt like dragging up a chair and watching him sleep, but I went out to the garage and got some wire and pliers and rigged a sort of latch on the door Freddy Russel had broken.

Then I went into the kitchen and poured myself a glass of milk. The house felt strange to me, like it wasn't mine anymore. It was no longer sanctuary. It had been invaded. I felt like a rape victim. Violated. Our house was no longer private, full of our spirits, thoughts, even our arguments. It was nothing more than a thing of glass, wood and brick that any thug with a crowbar or a screwdriver could bust open.

The milk tasted like chalk and rested mercury-heavy in my stomach. I poured the rest down the drain and went to bed.

Ann was asleep, and I was grateful for that. I had feared she would insist on a mercy fuck; sexual first aid. She worked that way sometimes, and I hated it. She meant well by it, but that didn't make me like it. Tonight I would have despised it, no matter how much I loved her or how enticing she might be.

I lay there looking at the ceiling, listening to Ann breathe. My stomach kept churning the milk around and around, and an instant replay of what had happened earlier was whirling endlessly through my head: swirls of shadow and muffled sounds, a flashlight, revolver steel, the wind from a bullet against my ear, the report of my own gun, the lights going on, the empty eye socket, blood and brains on the landscape painting and the very wall on which we taped our yearly Christmas cards.

It wasn't until daylight that I felt like sleeping.

4.

I could have slept in, but I didn't. I got up, dressed for work and went into the kitchen to sit at the table with Ann and Jordan.

Jordan was playing with his food, as usual. Seldom did a morning pass without some sort of fight between me and the boy, or between the boy and his mother. Something to do with the way he ate, or playing at the table. The kid couldn't get out of the house until he had spilled his milk. It was like a morning ritual that had to be observed.

And there were thousands of little things he did that made me climb the wall, and it was the same for Ann. She and I went through each day joyful for him and mad as hell at him, trying to figure if we were overly demanding of a four-year-old, or if he was a real-life Dennis the Menace. Or worse, some sort of criminal in the making, created by us, seasoned by our impatience and anger, tempered by his genetics, having acquired all the things we hated about ourselves, and none of the things we prized.

I thought too, each night as I went to bed, that no matter how hard I tried, it wasn't good enough. I never missed a day yelling at the little guy, or losing my temper in some way, and I certainly told him no more often than yes. Though I tried to listen to him

13

describing what the Pink Panther and Woody Woodpecker and the Pokey Puppy did, there were times when his little voice was like chalk on a blackboard and I would tune out his enthusiasms, and I knew he could sense it.

Then too, there was the other child, the one I thought about more often than I ever expected. The one Ann had carried inside her for eight and a half months and I had felt move inside her and had heard gurgling around in there when I put my ear to her stomach. The same child that filled her with poison and sent her to the hospital for days and prompted the late-night phone call in which she told me, "Our baby is dead," and then began to cry.

They used drugs to make her deliver, then offered us the body. A little girl. They said if we didn't want her they would autopsy the body for research and dispose of it. Later, I found out if we had asked for her they would have handed her to us in a black garbage bag.

At times I thought we should have at least looked at her. Maybe given her a name and had her buried. Other times I felt we had done the right thing. But right or wrong, the face of the child I never saw came to me in my dreams; a cold, gray face with its eyes open, and the eyes were like Ann's, bright, bright green. And I would awake. Sweating.

Sometimes I would drive by the hospital and see dark clouds, hanging over it, clouds that seemed full of storm. But I would know that it was smoke from the black incinerators out back; incinerators where placentas and lab experiments were disposed. And I wondered if my unnamed child had gone there after autopsy. Just so much ruined meat in a black garbage bag, cooked to past done, transformed to soot that would cling to the hospital roof and outside walls.

And when I dreamed or thought these things, I would always think of Jordan and wonder how he put up with my inadequacies as a father. Times like that, I felt like a bad actor masquerading as a parent in a school play.

I determined that this morning I would let nothing he did irritate me. It was the millionth time I had turned over that leaf in my mind. Each time I had failed to live up to it, but like some sort of Zen exercise, I thought repetition might make it easier for me eventually. And after what had happened last night, I saw the world in an entirely new and vulnerable light. It was just good to see the boy sitting there with his cereal, and as always, I took a secret pride in seeing my features on his little face. His hair was blond like his mother's, but the almond shape of his eyes, the prominence of the lips, the cleft in his chin, were mine.

Looking at him now, I hoped I was more of a presence in his life than my father had been in mine, and I hoped I wouldn't haunt him the way my father haunted me. That when it was all said and done he would have more than some uncertain memories and that there would be more between us than Christmas cards from distant cities with "love" written at the bottom.

I leaned out of my chair, kissed and hugged the boy. "Good morning, big guy."

"What was all that racket about last night, Daddy?" Racket was his new word. He used it every chance he got.

"Some people we had over."

"Why?"

"We needed them."

"Why?"

"Just for some things."

"What things?"

"Nothing much. You like that cereal?"

"Yeah."

It was some sort of processed, multicolored junk filled with too much sugar and air. I felt like hell for letting him have that garbage, but his mother liked it too, and there were those damn television commercials that offered toys and games inside, and that fueled him for it, and like so many parents, I had my weak moments. But I determined then and there that next time we went shopping we would come home with oatmeal and granola, eggs and bacon, a variety of fruits. Compliments of Richard Dane, part-time killer, full-time father.

"Taste?" Jordan asked.

I dipped my spoon into the mess and brought it back full of bright animal shapes. It tasted like shit.

"See," Jordan said. "It's good. You can get a fwizbee with one bogs top."

"That right?"

"Uh huh."

"You finish the cereal, then we'll send off the box top. Maybe you can start having some oatmeal when this is gone. Wouldn't that be good for a change? Oatmeal."

"I don't like oatmeal."

"Some eggs. Maybe some sausage."

"I don't like that neither. Just seerul."

I nodded, not wishing to argue, but grateful I had gotten his mind off the police. I was even more grateful he hadn't awakened last night and seen the dead man on the couch.

"You going to work?" Ann asked.

She could see that I was shaved and dressed, but she was giving me an invitation to stay home. It was an idea that did not appeal to me, however. Being in the house all day with her gone and Jordan at day school would just cause me to replay last night endlessly in my head. Everytime I looked at the couch or at the brighter spot on the wall where the painting had hung, it would come back to me.

"Sure, I'm going."

"Feel like it?"

"Close enough. It's better than staying here."

"Did you sleep?"

"Some."

"Sorry I was asleep when you came to bed."

"That's all right. I was too tired anyway."

"That's why you go to bed, Daddy, 'cause you're tired," Jordan said.

I smiled at him. "You're right. I should have known that."

"I know everythang," he said.

I winked at Ann.

"What you doing with your eye, Daddy?"

"Something in it."

"Gid it out?"

"Think so."

Jordan turned back to his breakfast, and I found there really was something in my eyes.

Tears.

I excused myself before they could notice, went to the bathroom, washed my face and stared in the mirror. I thought maybe I should see a different face looking back at me, but it was the same goon I saw in there every day. Killing a man had not altered my appearance in the least. I still looked like a fairly healthy, not too bad-looking, starting to bald, thirty-five-year-old man.

Jordan appeared in the doorway.

"God to go bad."

"Come in."

"You gid out."

I patted him on the head, closed the door and went out. The tears started again. Goddamn, I'd never been this weepy before. But then it hit me what the tears were all about. It wasn't just that I had killed a man. It was that I was suddenly aware of Jordan's mortality. I had accepted my own some time back, but not his. After the loss of the first child I felt that I had paid my dues. But I knew now that was ridiculous. There are no such things as dues. Nothing's promised.

I got to thinking about what might have happened had Ann not heard the noise and alerted me. What if Jordan had heard the sound, got up to investigate, wandered into the living room in his feeted Superman pajamas, clutching his teddy bear?

A grim scenario formed in my mind. The burglar hearing Jordan, turning, drawing the gun, firing without consideration, a red blossom opening in my son's chest....

I heard the toilet flush, and I went into our bedroom and closed the door, sat on the edge of the bed and hoped Jordan wouldn't come in. I tried to dismiss all thoughts of mortality from my mind, my family's mortality and my own. I sat there for a few minutes until the lie of permanence and absolute happiness was once again real enough to hold and my inner eye was blind enough not to see it slipping between my fingers like sand.

5.

After Ann left for work, I let Jordan watch a few minutes of cartoons while I had a last cup of coffee, then I drove him to his day school at the Baptist church and took myself to work.

I parked behind my frame shop and got out. It was only eight-thirty and the air was already sticky. July in East Texas is like that. The trees hold the heat and smother you with it. Sometimes it's so bad the humidity seems to have weight, and walking through it is like trying to wade through gelatin.

I stood by my car and breathed in the warm, small-town air. In spite of the heat, it was times like this that I was glad I lived in a town of forty thousand (counting ten thousand transient college students) instead of a place like Houston. Ann and I had lived there briefly when we were newly married, and we hated it. It was ugly, hurried and depressing. And there was all that crime.

Crime. That was a hoot. Even a small town like LaBorde wasn't free of that. Just ask me, the burglar killer.

I got my key and went in the back and started coffee. At eight-forty-five the hired help showed. Valerie and James.

Valerie is a bright, attractive woman and a good frame builder, if a little impatient with customers. James, on the other hand, is a so-so frame builder, and a master at knowing what the customer really wants. But he hasn't figured out what Valerie wants. She snubs him. He spends a lot of his time with his eyes stuck to her ass, like a mountain climber mooning over a cherished but unattainable summit.

I hoped plenty of work would come in today so I could stay busy, and maybe not have to talk too much. I knew if I talked very long about anything, I'd talk about last night, and I didn't want to do that. Word would get around soon enough without my help. There hadn't been any reporters last night, but it would certainly make the paper, if only in the abbreviated crime report section of the *LaBorde Daily*, which is as close to being a real newspaper as a water hose is to being a snake.

While Valerie and James poured themselves cups of coffee, I went up front, turned the Closed sign around to Open and unlocked the door.

About nine-thirty Ann called during her break at the high school.

"Just a minute," I said. I glanced at James and Valerie in the back of the shop. Valerie was working on a frame. She was bent over the table giving James a nice view of her buns; the red dress she wore was stretched over them tight as a bongo skin. James was gesticulating wildly, giving her a line of prattle between flashes of his teeth and puffs of his cigarette. I was somehow reminded of The Little Engine That Could. "Go ahead," I said.

"You doing okay?" Ann asked.

"I'm not in the mood for a parade or anything. But yeah, I guess I'm all right. How about you?"

"I'm getting off next period to go talk to the police. Richard, it's all over school. I don't know how, but it is. Some of the teachers have asked me about it. I tried to talk to them, but I couldn't communicate too well. Even some of the kids have asked."

"Shit. Maybe you should go home."

"Got to deal with it sometime, and I guess now is as good a time as any.... You're sure you're okay?"

"Fine," I lied.

"All right. I got to go, baby. Love you."

"You too."

About ten-thirty Jack Crow, the mailman, showed up. He came in out of the July heat and it seemed to follow him, hung in the doorway like warm dog breath for a full fifteen seconds.

Jack is one of those big men who thinks his size, rugged face and disregard for intellectuals makes him a man. He can't just deliver the mail and say hello, he's got to spend a few minutes each morning making catty remarks to Valerie about how he likes redheads, and how she's a looker, all the usual routines men like Jack think are charming. He also likes to talk about his hunting, fishing and war experiences. To hear him tell it, Hemingway was a perch fisher and Audie Murphy was a windup soldier. And he's the real thing.

"Man, that air-conditioning feels good," he said. "Cushy job you got here, folks. But tell you, wouldn't trade. Mine keeps me in shape." He slapped his stomach. "Course," he said looking at Valerie, "you look in shape."

"TV dinners," she said.

He laughed. It sounded like something strangling. Well, one could hope.

He came over to the counter and leaned on it and looked me square in the eyes, like we were secret comrades, but said loudly, "I hear you got you one last night."

The bottom fell out of my stomach. I knew it had to happen, but the fact that the first person who brought it up to me was Macho Jack seemed like cruel and unusual punishment. I didn't know what to say back so I didn't say anything. Jack was doing all the talking anyway.

"Mack over at the newspaper told me. Said you shot that sonofabitch right in the eye, killed him deader than an anvil. Was it a nigger? Wetback?"

Valerie and James stopped working and came over to the desk.

"What's all this?" James asked.

"Dick got him one last night," Jack said.

First of all, I hated being called Dick. It's the nickname for a man's sexual equipment, and as far as I'm concerned you might as well call me Prick. And I sure didn't like Jack calling me that; I wouldn't want that bastard to call me to dinner.

"He shot the bastard right through the head," Jack said, not waiting for me to answer. "Killed his ass."

"That's enough," I said.

"No need to be modest, Dicky." Dicky? "Hell, I'd be proud. Sonofabitch breaks into my house he better be ready to pick his teeth out of his asshole. I keep a pump 12-gauge right under the bed, and if—"

"Drop it, Jack," I said. "Just drop it."

"It's nothing to be ashamed of," Jack said. "If it were me—"

"It wasn't you. It was me. And I'm not ashamed of it, just not proud of it either. You got some mail for me, leave it. If not, get out."

Jack's face turned red and his mouth went slack. "You kill some asshole, and you get to talking pretty damn tough. Think you're fucking Clint Eastwood."

"Just leave," I said.

"All right, cowboy." Jack reached into his bag and tossed a handful of letters on the counter. They slid off and fell on the floor. "Enjoy your fucking mail, Dicky."

He gave me a parting glare and stomped out, holding the door open long enough to let in some of July. "Hope your fucking air-conditioner goes out," he said.

"And I hope a rabid dog chews off your nuts," Valerie said.

James and I both jerked our heads toward her. Valerie?

Jack stood in the doorway, shocked. "That's not very ladylike," he managed.

"You got it," Valerie said.

Jack swallowed, let go of the door, and walked away. He looked back through the showcase window just before he was out of sight, and Valerie shot him the finger.

Valerie looked at us and blushed redder than her dress. "Well," she said, "I just don't like him."

6.

I told James and Valerie the whole story and they were good about it. They didn't ask for any gory details. I finally left things in their hands and drove over to Kelly's. I just didn't want to talk about it anymore or be around anyone that knew about it for a while. I needed, as they say in California, some space. Or as we say in Texas, I wanted to be left the hell alone.

I passed Jack on the sidewalk on the way over there. He was still making his rounds. He had his head down and was walking furiously. I thought about how Valerie had put him down, and I almost honked at him so I could remind him, but I didn't. My sense of humor wasn't up to it.

Kelly's is an old-fashioned café on the west side of town, and I eat there often. I like it because it reminds me of my high school days. I'm not the type that lives in the past, but I don't mind thinking about it some. I used to take dates to Kelly's and we'd drink malts and eat hamburgers there. It was actually owned by a man named Kelly then. But that was quite a few years back. He was out at the LaBorde Cemetery now, holding up a plastic flower arrangement.

I couldn't go into Kelly's without thinking about Stud Franklin who went in there one Saturday and shot himself through the head with a .22 pistol. I didn't see it, but I heard about it from plenty who did. He just walked in there and, said, "Fuck him and his pig too," and put the gun to his head. He was upset because he didn't win the FHA contest. He'd raised a pig for it, worked all year on that pig and put all his money into it, bought fancy food and medical supplies. He was beat out by some backwoods farmer who raised his pig on stale bread and cakes and fed him chewing tobacco to kill worms. Later, they found Stud's pig hung up in the fancy concrete pen Stud had built for him. No one suspected the pig of suicide. Stud had seemed stable up until then.

And the back booth, the one with the rip in the leather that had been badly taped over and over for years, was where my first real romance ended. I had put my hand on Kathy Counsel's knee and tried to slide it up under her dress for a better prize and she had slapped me, the sound of that slap went through the place like a mortar shot. I went out of there with her yelling at me and the other kids laughing, and I didn't go back in there for a month. Kathy Counsel got knocked up about six months later by our star quarterback, Herschel Roman, and they had to quit school and Herschel threw his last ball and started throwing nozzles into gas tanks down at the Fina on Main. He was still there. He owned the place now and he watched lots of football on the TV next to the Coke machine. Kathy had gotten fat and had a tongue sharp as a meat fork. Their kid played football and was bad at it and hated it, or so the rumor went. Occasionally, I had the urge to call up Kathy and thank her for that slap.

Out back of Kelly's was where I had my only two fights. Lost both of them. I couldn't even remember what they were over. They had both been with my best high school friend, Jerry Quail. He got drafted after graduation because he wasn't college material. He never saw action in Nam. The week before he went over there he fell out of a helicopter on maneuvers and was killed. I attended the funeral.

I didn't take one of the booth seats. I sat down at the counter and Kay came over. She was the only waitress in the place that time of day, and I liked her. She was pretty in a peroxide, too-muchmakeup sort of way, and happily married or not, I couldn't help but enjoy the way her hips worked beneath that starched white outfit she wore. She had some of what Valerie had; an element women wished they could buy bottled and so did their men.

I smiled best I could and ordered coffee. She poured it up and said, "I heard what happened."

"Christ," I said. "People in this town are goddamn telepathic."

"They just have big mouths," she said. "Anyway, I'm sorry. I'm sure it's tough."

"That was just the right thing to say, Kay. Thanks."

She smiled and I moved over to a booth. I sat with my head back against the old, red, leather cushion and closed my eyes. Immediately last night jumped through my head.

I opened my eyes and drank half of my coffee in one gulp. It was bitter. I called to Kay to bring me a Coke. I sipped it. It wasn't any better.

"Use your phone?"

Kay was behind the bar wiping up a water spot. "Have at it. You know where it is."

I went through the back door, into the stockroom. The phone was sitting on the directory on a shelf next to an economy-sized can of tomatoes. That would be for the chili they served. Good stuff, but hot as a potbellied stove.

I leaned on the shelf and used the directory to look up a number. It was on the first page in big letters. I dialed.

"LaBorde Police Department"

"I'd like to speak to Lieutenant Price."

"Just a moment."

When Price came on the line, I said, "This is Dane. I just wanted to know what happened to Russel's body."

"He'll be buried day after tomorrow. Would have been today, but they did an autopsy."

"Why?"

"Fairly standard procedure. Why do you want to know about burial?"

"This Russel, he got any family besides his old man?"

"I don't think so. None that we know of. The county is paying for it. A pauper's funeral we call it."

"Where's he going to be buried?"

"Greenley's Cemetery. You're not planning on coming, are you?"

"It crossed my mind."

"Guilt?"

"Something like that."

"I know how you feel, but you're letting this get out of hand. You've got to accept the fact that you killed him in self-defense. He broke into your house."

"Just got to thinking about it. Doesn't seem right he'll be buried without anyone there."

"You think his spirit's going to feel cheerier with you there? The man who killed him?"

I was quiet for a moment. When Price spoke again, his words seemed packed in ice. "Look, I'm not trying to make you feel shitty, okay? I'm just saying there's no point. I doubt if he'd killed you he'd be attending your funeral."

"Not the point—"

"Maybe it is the point. Just do your best to forget it. Get on with your life. People are going to talk about it and you're going to hear it. It'll be rough for a while. But it'll pass."

"What time are they burying him?"

"You're stubborn, aren't you?"

"Just humor me, Price. I don't know I'm going to do anything, but it would make me feel better to know. Day after tomorrow when?"

Price sighed. "One-thirty. But Dane, do yourself a favor. Stay away."

I hung up and dialed a good friend of mine who's a house painter, gritted my teeth and told him what had happened. I tried to make it simple and clear.

"Hell, Richard, I'm sorry."

"No need to be," I said. "It's done. Look, what I need is for you to paint my living room. It's not that there's still blood on the wall, but it would make me feel better to have a fresh coat on the room."

"I understand, I'll get my boys and we'll be over there about noon."

"Thanks, Ted. And I'm calling a locksmith and the furniture store. You beat any of them there, let them in. Best way for you to get in is to take some wire pliers and go around back and cut through the wire rig I made last night."

"No problem," Ted said.

"Thanks."

I used the book again and got the number of a furniture store.

"I want a couch," I said, and I gave them the colors of the room, the general dimensions. They described what they had and I picked. I hoped Ann would like it well enough. Buying it sight unseen was not a good idea, but I just didn't want to deal with people face to face any more than I had to.

"When can you deliver? I'd like it today if you could."

"That will be fine. About one o'clock all right?"

"That's good. There'll be a painter there named Ted Lawson to let you in. Could you take my old couch off my hands? It's not good for anything, but I'll pay you extra to carry it off."

He thought on that a moment. "I suppose we can do that. No charge."

"Good. And could you cover the new one with plastic? I don't want to get paint on it."

He said they could, and I hung up, then dialed the locksmith.

"Truman's Locks, Truman speaking."

"My name is Richard Dane, and—"

"You're the fella shot that burglar last night, ain't you?"

Great Godalmighty, word sure did move.

"That's right. I need a lock on the door he tore up. Can you do it today?"

"I can start today. Depends on how bad the door is busted. You might have to get someone out there to fix that first."

"It just needs a lock," I said.

"All right. Hey, they gonna put you in jail?"

"It was self-defense."

"That don't mean nothing these days. You can't trust the cops any better than the crooks. What's that address?"

I told him.

"Say, Mr. Dane. How about a burglar alarm and some burglar bars? I could fix you up real good. Goddamn Houdini couldn't get in your house once I got you secured."

I knew he was working on my paranoia, and I knew I'd regret it later, but last night was still too close. "Yeah," I said. "Let's shoot the works."

"Good move. We'll get that lock and the bars in today. Start on that alarm system tomorrow. That sound okay?"

"Peachy," I said, and hung up.

I went up front and sat at my booth again and finished my Coke. It tasted a little better. I looked at the clock behind the counter and over the mirror. Eleven. Too early for lunch.

To hell with that.

"Kay," I called, "how about you get that cook in back to fix me up a fried egg sandwich, and don't hold the grease."

"Got it," she said, then yelled to the back. "Clyde."

A black man in a stained white apron appeared at the cook window. "Two baby chicks, dead on bread and don't hold the grease," she said.

Clyde tapped two fingers to his forehead in salute and disappeared. I heard grease splattering in a pan a little later.

COLD IN JULY

Kay came over with a Lone Star beer and sat it on the table. "On the house," she said.

I took my time drinking the beer, and later eating the sandwich, listened to a couple of Dwight Yoakam songs on the jukebox, then drove back to the shop.

7.

A few people who had heard about the killing came into the shop, and at least one of them was nothing more than a morbid curiosity seeker. He didn't even try to pretend he had business there, he just wanted to know about last night. I told him all I felt like telling him, then went to the bathroom in the back and stayed there until James and Valerie got rid of him.

Rest of the day I worked on frames by myself and had James and Valerie stay up front. There wasn't that much work for them up there, and I really could have used one of them on the frames, but I wanted to be left alone and I wanted to stay away from bullshit conversation. Talk about the weather and the Dallas Cowboys wasn't going to cut it today. It would only remind me I was putting up a veneer against the real concerns, and that would be worse.

About four-thirty I was working on a limited-edition print, putting 100 percent rag mat around it, when the phone rang. James answered and said it was for me.

It was Price.

"There may be a problem," he said.

"What kind of problem?"

"Ben Russel. Freddy's father. He got out of Huntsville yesterday. He knows his son is dead, knows he was killed in a burglary, and word is he's coming to the funeral. He could be dangerous. Don't go to the funeral."

"I'll think about it."

"Stay away from Ben Russel, Mr. Dane. He's dangerous. You being at his son's funeral would just make matters worse. You stay home and maybe he'll just let things be and move on. He probably doesn't care one way or another about the boy. His type is vengeful. Just looking for an excuse."

"Thanks for the advice, Price."

"Heed it, Dane. Trust me on this."

I hung up and went back to my matting. I backed the print and got a piece of no-glare glass for it, but found I couldn't make it fit the frame. My hands didn't work right.

I had James finish it. I drank a cup of coffee I didn't need, then went to the bathroom to think. I tried to picture Ben Russel and imagined him long and lean with a crew cut and a scar on the side of his face. I figured he had a gravelly voice and was the kind of guy that had killed a fellow inmate in prison with a spoon he had sharpened in metal shop. I could imagine the warden talking to him when they let him out, telling him, "Go straight, Russel," And I could imagine Russel thinking, "Yeah, soon as I finish a little job in LaBorde."

I washed my face and went home early.

8.

Ann picks Jordan up from day school every day when she gets off work, so when I got home he was sitting at the table eating a bologna sandwich. Mayonnaise was dripping out of it and there was a circle of the stuff thick as mad dog foam around his mouth. The mayonnaise jar and the table were covered with it too.

"Hi, Daddy."

"Hi, son."

I looked at the table and the spoon and the jar and went over and got a paper towel and cleaned up best I could. I made a point of not saying anything to him about the mess. Usually I jumped him. But I was trying to put things in better perspective this day, and suddenly the mess seemed a lot less major than it might have the day before. And for that matter, who was I to cast the first stone? I wasn't that neat and organized now, and I was thirty-five.

I saw that Ted and his boys were in the living room, painting away. They had the floor covered in plastic sheets, but there was very little splashed on it. They had their backs to me, and as I had come in through the garage, they hadn't noticed me yet. I watched them work a minute, then looked at my watch. Six o'clock. That was one good thing about hiring a man who worked for himself. He worked until the job got done, not until five o'clock. Besides, a painter had to take work where he could find it. They didn't get the offer on a daily basis.

I kissed Jordan on the head and he told me a story his teacher had read the class that day. It was about Clifford the Big Red Dog. He liked the story a lot. He retold it loudly and with lots of gestures. During this time Ted and his sons turned to look and I gave them a nod. When Jordan finished his story, I poured him a fresh glass of milk to spill, and went into the living room for a full view of the work.

They looked to be about finished. The room was strong with the smell of paint, a smell I normally despised, but today it seemed fresh as a spring morning. And the old couch was gone. The new one was in the center of the room covered with a plastic sheet as I had instructed.

Ted wiped his hands on a rag he had in his back pocket and came over. "I'd shake," he said, "but I might get some paint on you. We'll be out of your hair in about an hour or so. If you can keep your boy off the wall, it'll look better than new soon as it's completely dry."

"I'll do my best," I said.

"Locksmith came by. He put the bill in the kitchen."

"I didn't see it," I said.

"It's stuck to your refrigerator with one of those fruit magnets. I looked. He overcharged you. He said he'd be back tomorrow to try and finish. And, you can see the couch came."

"Yeah."

"You're all right, I suppose?"

"Sure."

"Well, get so you think you aren't, give me a call. Hell, remember how we used to talk about things in high school? I'm still here. We ought to just get together for a beer anyway. It's been a long time."

"You're right, it has."

Ted went back to work and I went over to the door to look at the lock. It was pretty serious looking. Good. And there was a sliding grillwork that could be pulled across the glass at night and locked in place, just in case a rhino charged you. I didn't know if I felt secure or stupid. The only thing I knew for certain was I wasn't going to mention Ben Russel to Ann, least not now.

I got the portable television out of the storage closet in the kitchen, put it on the drainboard and plugged it in. I tuned in Bugs Bunny and left Jordan watching that and drinking the milk he hadn't spilled yet.

I found Ann in the bedroom, sitting on the edge of the bed, her back to me. Her elbows were on her knees and her hands were supporting her head as if it had grown too heavy. I closed the door and sat down beside her.

"I hate the couch," she said.

"Sorry. I can take it back."

"You should have asked me what I wanted. Don't we always do that? We want something, we make up our minds together. Right?"

"I just wanted the other one out of the house."

"You could have waited on a new one until I could look with you."

"I'm not thinking clearly."

"It wasn't very considerate of you."

"I'll have them take it back. Could we talk about something besides the couch?"

"I just don't like it, that's all."

"You talk to the police?" I asked.

"You're changing the subject, but yes, I talked to them. Lieutenant Price was very nice. It went quickly."

"Want to go out to dinner?"

"Jordan made himself a sandwich."

"I thought maybe Dorothy could keep him. She owes us a baby-sitting, doesn't she? What say just you and I go? Mexican food maybe."

"I can call her and see."

"Good. I'll wash up and shave. I feel sort of grungy."

"Brush your teeth too. Your breath has hair on it.... Do you really think we need bars on the doors and windows? Alarms? Did you see that bill?"

"No, I haven't seen the bill. But right now, the way I feel, I wish I could put this house on Mars." I got up and started out.

"Richard. I still don't like that couch. It looks like it was designed by that guy who did the sets for *Alien*."

"It goes tomorrow," I said.

After dinner, we picked up Jordan and got him to bed early, and Ann and I made love. It was good. Our sex life had never turned bitter, but it had turned quick, spaced between too many obligations and performed far too often when we felt the least like it.

But this wasn't like that. It was like the old times when we couldn't wait to get at each other. It reminded me of college and the back of my old battered '61 Ford; worn out when I got it, worn out more by my neglect. We used to do all our loving in the backseat of that car at the drive-in because we both had strict dorms and roommates. I remembered that Ford with the sort of reverence a monk reserves for a shrine.

I lay there with Ann asleep on my arm and looked at the space between the curtains and saw one of the burglar bars banded against the window glass like a strip of cancer across a pale eye. I looked at the bar until I made it go away. I made everything go away. I imagined us in the backseat of the old Ford with pieces of ripped roof cloth dangling down like limp stalactites. It was a cold December night, not the dead of July, and Ann and I had the old patchwork quilt across us and the Ford's windows were all frosted.

I lay there believing that for a long duration, traveling backwards by mental time machine to a time when all was right with the world and I thought Ann and I would live forever and that our future would always be as bright as the chrome on a brand-new Buick.

9.

So the next day the alarms were installed and the couch went back and Ann and I picked a new one. And by the next day I was able to tell myself it was time to get on with life, and it was foolish of me to consider seeing Russel buried. That wouldn't make things any better, and I just might see his old man, and I didn't need that.

But on the other hand, what if no one went to the funeral but the grave diggers? That didn't seem right either. Even the executioner would be more welcome, I thought. I had at least seen his face, and it was a face that would be branded on my memory forever.

Still, I wasn't going. And I wasn't going all the while I drove over there, telling myself I was only driving by. And I wasn't going when I parked under some oaks across the blacktop from the graveyard, and I wasn't going when I got out of my car and leaned on it, looked across at the burying.

It wasn't funeral weather. It was hot and gummy. The oaks I was under didn't provide much relief. It was as if they were dripping hot ink instead of shadow, but I knew if I stood out of that shadow, out in the bright sunlight, it would be even worse;

molten honey. For this kind of business it should have been rainy and cold and the graveyard should have been full of people dressed in black, at least some of them crying. But it wasn't like that for Freddy Russel.

What he got were two grave diggers, and a hired preacher waiting impatiently beside the cemetery fence in a bright, black Buick with the door open fanning himself with what looked like a church tract, which was probably its best use.

The grave was already dug, most likely the day before, and there was a contraption over the hole that was used to crank the coffin down. One of the grave diggers wore a Hawaiian shirt with red and yellow parrots on it. He and the other man were laughing about something, probably an off-color joke about preachers, and they worked very fast, cranking at the rig, lowering Freddy down. For all they cared the coffin could have been empty.

When they had the coffin in the hole they waved the preacher over, and the preacher stood by the grave and cracked his Bible and started reading. When he finished, he said a few words, and damn few at that, and wrapped it up with an "amen." The whole thing had all the conviction of a hooker's lovemaking. The preacher checked his watch and made for the Buick, cranked it, and he was out of there. Probably had a late free lunch somewhere.

I was about to follow suit when an old, blue Ambassador drove up next to the cemetery fence and a big guy got out and stood beside it watching the grave diggers toss dirt on the box. He lit a cigarette, turned and saw me. He looked to be in his late fifties, slightly paunchy, but handsome in a workingman sort of way. He stood there smoking his cigarette and staring at me, then he gave up on the smoke, put a heel to it, and started across the road.

As he neared, I saw that he was older than I first thought. Perhaps his late sixties. But it hadn't hurt him much. His face had the look of a comfortable, old shoe, and there was something about the way he walked that defied age; weary confidence preceded him like the figurehead of a great ship.

"You're Dane aren't you?" he asked as he came to my side of the road.

My pulse quickened. I knew who he was, though he wasn't the fantasy image I had conjured two days before.

"Yeah, you're Dane," he said, answering his own question. "You know me?"

"I've got a hunch," I said.

"I know you. I've made a point of it. When I came to town, first thing I did was ask around. People told me what I wanted to know. Said you got your picture in the papers a lot. Good citizen stuff. I went to the newspapers and asked to see their morgue, said I was interested in local history, said I was a writer researching a book. I saw your picture in quite a few issues. Big man here in LaBorde, Dane. And by the way. You take a good picture."

"It won't make it any better for you, but I didn't want to kill your son. I had to."

"You're right. I don't feel any better. Good of you to come out though, so you could see the shit go into the hole. Real nice of you."

"He broke into my house, for God's sake. He had a gun. He tried to kill me. I shot him in self-defense."

"I don't think that sounds like him. He was my only son."

"I'm sorry."

"That tidies it up. I feel better already, you having said you're sorry. You have a son, don't you?"

I felt a tingle at the base of my skull, as if some kind of cold borer worm were working itself inside my head.

"Ought to be about four now. I read the birth announcement. Nice name, Jordan. And I like your wife's name too. I had an aunt named Ann. She got hit by a truck."

"Russel, listen to me—"

"People around town I've talked to say your boy looks a lot like you, that he's really something. God, wouldn't it be awful if something happened to him?"

"Is that some kind of threat, you sonofabitch?"

"Not at all. I was just saying it would be awful if something happened to him. It could, you know? Look what happened to my son."

"Maybe if you'd been a better father, it wouldn't have happened."

"You have no idea what kind of father I was."

"I can imagine. You stay away from my son. My family. Hear me?"

"Don't shit yourself, Dane. I was just pointing out how horrible it would be if something happened to your little Jordan. Little kids don't always watch what they do. You have to be very careful with them. They get hurt easy. Killed sometimes."

"Come near my family, and I'll kill you."

He smiled at me and got out a cigarette and lit it. He pushed the pack toward me. "Smoke?" I noticed his hands were exactly like my father's. Thick and square and powerful. It made me uncomfortable.

"I meant what I said, Russel."

As I opened my car door and slid behind the wheel, he said, "Have a nice day, sonny boy."

10.

"I told you to stay away from there," Price said.

We were in the police assembly room, which served as a kind of lounge, and like everything else about the station, it surprised me. It was cool and clean. The vending machines were well stocked.

Price looked his usual sharp self. Today he wore a gray suit with a maroon shirt and striped tie, and his shoes were as shiny as ever.

"I know," I said. "But he wouldn't have left me alone if I'd stayed home. He's been asking around about me. Even went to the newspaper morgue to read about me, saw pictures so he could identify me."

Price ran a hand over his face as if trying to reshape it. "Anyone overhear you two?"

"No."

"Tell me exactly what he said."

I did.

"It wouldn't have mattered if the two of you were overheard. No real threat there. He even told you to have a nice day."

"It's the way he said it."

"You got zip. Maybe if someone could testify that the tone of his voice was threatening, you might have something, but not much. Besides, you haven't got anyone."

"Can I get protection for my family?"

"Officially he hasn't done anything."

"He's an ex-con."

"He served his time.... Look, I believe he threatened you, I do. But it doesn't amount to anything officially. I don't make all the decisions around here either. Even if I wanted to post someone to watch your family I haven't got a legal reason to do it. If you're lucky, he'll go away. He could just be worked up over things. That's natural. No crime in seeing the man who killed your son. If he wanted to harm you, he could have done that at the cemetery."

"It isn't me he wants, it's my son. An eye for an eye, a tooth for a tooth...a son for a son."

"All right, listen up tight, Mr. Dane. Unofficially, I can give you protection for a couple of days. It might get my ass in a crack, but I'll do it. It's possible the chief will pull me off of it if he finds out, but we'll give it a shot, even if I have to do it myself. I'll have a car watch your place, and we'll check with you from time to time."

"You said a couple of days. That's all you can do?"

"Two days, Mr. Dane. That's it."

"And what if he waits until the third day?"

"He makes a real threat you can prove, we'll move in on him. I'll run a check on him in the meantime, and my suggestion to you is to get another gun, sleep light, and hope he leaves town. I think there's a good chance he will."

"I don't find that too goddamn reassuring. You said he was dangerous. You're punishing me for not listening to you."

"That's stupid. He is dangerous. But I can't do a thing unless he tries something. Innocent until proven guilty, Mr. Dane."

46

"When does this protection begin?"

"Tonight. That's as soon as I can arrange it. I can't make a big deal out of it. We're short-manned as it is."

"In LaBorde?"

"More goes on here than you think, Mr. Dane. A lot more. I want you to describe his car. If you're lucky, he stole it. That would be something to hold him on, and with him being an ex-con, it would be a quick trip back to the pen. Perhaps for good this time."

I didn't know the license plate number, but I gave him a good description of the car, for what that was worth. There must have been a lot of old, blue Ambassadors around.

Though I didn't much feel like it, I shook Price's hand and went outside. I understood his position, but I didn't much care for it.

Standing there on the edge of the parking lot, I thought about Russel and his son and tried to imagine them at home together; Ben on the floor playing with little Freddy, or maybe sitting around in his bathrobe Christmas morning, laughing while the boy unwrapped his presents. But these weren't visions I could hang onto. I could more easily imagine him teaching the boy to beat a lock or hotwire a car.

Then I got to thinking about what Russel had said about my son, and I got mad again, then scared. I drove over to the day school on North Street to get Jordan early. I planned to call Ann from there and tell her I had him and where she could meet us.

When I pulled into the church parking lot I saw Russel's Ambassador and Russel was standing over by the dumpster, smoking a cigarette.

I parked near his car, got out, made a point of memorizing the license plate this time, and went over to him.

Russel looked at his watch. "I didn't think your boy got out until three-forty-five."

I swung at him with everything I had. He rolled his head like a boxer to avoid it, but I caught him some on the jaw and the punch was hard enough to move his head and send his cigarette flying out of his mouth.

I brought the left around and tried to coldcock him, but he blocked that with his right forearm and stepped back out of range of any more blows.

"You hit pretty hard for a frame builder, Dane. You got to watch dropping your shoulder and roundhousing though. Gives your punch away, takes half the sting out."

"You sonofabitch," I said.

"Could be," he said, and he got out a fresh cigarette and lit it. I stood there breathing heavy as I watched him take a puff and put the lighter back in his pocket. I watched to see if his hands were trembling. They weren't. But mine were.

"Been to the cops yet? That's what I figured you'd do. Go straight to them. I think you're of the opinion that I'm threatening you and your family."

I wanted to tear back into him, but he'd taken my shots so easily, I figured, sixty or not, he could mop up the parking lot with me.

"I told you once to stay away from my family. I won't tell you again."

"Careful, Dane," he said. "You keep threatening me like that, I may have to lodge a complaint."

I walked back to my car and drove it over to the far side of the lot and got out and walked through the side door. Once inside the glass door, I turned to see if he was still standing there.

He wasn't, and the Ambassador was gone.

11.

I left a message for Ann at the school, told the receptionist to tell her everything was all right and not to worry, but to meet Jordan and me at the police station.

At the station, Jordan was restless and I bought him a Coke and a package of those round peanut-butter-filled crackers. He drank some of the Coke and used the can to mash the crackers into the table. That seemed to bother Price. You would have thought it was his table. I didn't make Jordan stop.

"Who was there first?" Price asked. "You or Russel?"

"Russel."

"Did he do anything to you?"

"No. He said he thought my son got off at three-forty-five and I took a swing at him."

"Did you make contact?"

"Yeah."

"Did he hit you back?"

"No."

Price did the reshaping number with his hand and face again. "You still got nothing, Mr. Dane. The worst he could be accused of is loitering. That's a big parking lot. He could have been planning to go in one of the stores on the other side of it; maybe he was having a smoke before going inside. He could try and press charges against you for taking a swing at him. You've admitted yourself that you did."

I didn't even feel like arguing anymore. I could see where this was going. "For what it's worth," I said. "I got his license number."

"I'll run a check on the computer. Give me the number. It won't take but a minute."

I gave him the number and he went away with it and came back in about two minutes. I was watching the clock.

"Local car rental. All legal."

"I guess that leaves me where I was."

"I'm afraid so. I know how you feel, but I can't arrest a man on another's say-so. Even if the one accused is an ex-con. If we arrested everyone that might commit a crime, the jail would be full long before sundown."

"I get the picture. But you still intend to have someone watching the house tonight?"

"That's right."

I collected Jordan and we went outside to wait on Ann. Jordan told me a story about a little blue rabbit that could run fast, and about five minutes later Ann drove up. I told her to follow us to our favorite Mexican restaurant and I'd tell her the story there.

Ann went through all the arguments I had given Price, and I gave her all of Price's arguments back. She didn't like my answers any better than I had liked them coming from Price.

"I think you and Jordan should leave town," I said. "Stay somewhere until this blows over."

"I don't like that," Ann said.

"I don't want the idghalada, daddy, I want chips."

"It's enchilada, son, and don't talk when we're talking. It's not polite."

"But I don't want—"

"Will you hush, son? I'm trying to talk to your mother. Or she's trying to talk to me.... Christ, I don't remember who was talking to who."

"I just want chips," Jordan said.

"Eat the chips then," I said, "but let mommy and me talk."

Jordan started eating out of the bowl of corn chips, looking quite content with himself.

"I was saying," Ann said, "that I don't like that idea. I don't think we should leave. He could follow us. If we went to your mother's for example, and he did follow us, we could put her in jeopardy as well as ourselves. I say we do as Price suggested. We get a gun and watch out. We've got burglar alarms and bars now. That should be worth something."

"We could take Jordan out of school a few days," I said. "And maybe you could get some time off. I could let James and Valerie run the shop and we could all stay home for a time. Wait Russel out."

"It seems like the best idea to me," Ann said. "Let's go home."

12.

I drove out ahead of Ann, and Jordan rode with her. I began to relax some. I began to see everything in a different light. I felt silly. Just because Russel was trying to scare me, didn't mean he had the balls to do anything. It didn't necessarily mean anything more than he was upset about his son, which was normal. He was certainly no cream puff, I could see that, but he was still an old man and my house was barred and full of alarms and I had a shotgun in the garage and tough as he might be he couldn't eat lead, as they might say in a B gangster movie.

I thought about the shotgun. Like the pistol, it was something I had acquired more on the spur of the moment than by design.

About five years back, in a town close to LaBorde, some nut had broken into a house and killed a family while they slept. Two of the victims were kids. Ann was pregnant with Jordan at the time, and I guess I was overcome with paternal instincts. I had never owned a gun and had never wanted to, but I went out and bought the .38 that had eventually killed Russel. I told Ann's father about the .38 on a visit to Houston, and he had given me the shotgun, told me it was better than the revolver. Said it was less likely to penetrate walls and injure family members. It was a short-barreled Winchester pump, and he gave me some double aught loads and I took the shotgun and the shells home and they went into the garage and the pistol stayed in the shoe box. As my hysteria faded, I forgot about the shotgun and nearly forgot about the .38.

To the best of my memory the shotgun was broken down and was in the garage storage cabinet in the original box with oilcans and tools in front of it. I told myself I would get it out of the box when I got home and load it, put it under my bed, but in the end, I was certain I would feel silly with it there because nothing was going to come of my mental cowboy movie. Russel would lose interest in his dead son, as he had probably had little interest in him when he was alive, and he would go away and things would return to normal.

But when I pulled up in our drive and Ann and Jordan pulled in behind me, the fear and uncertainty returned. Even with the bars and the alarms, or perhaps because I had to have them, I knew I might never feel safe in that house again. And I was more certain of this when I went ahead of them with my key in hand ready to unlock the door.

It was cracked open about three inches already.

I turned and scooped Jordan up with one arm and grabbed Ann's elbow with the other and directed them back to Ann's car.

"Get in," I said.

"Richard?"

"We just got here, Daddy."

"Get behind the wheel, Ann. The front door is unlocked and open."

She gave me a strange look, then turned and opened the car door. I put Jordan inside and Ann climbed in behind the wheel.

"Get to the Ferguson's and call the police. Ask for Price."

"Come with us," Ann said.

"Git."

54

I closed the door and walked back toward the house. I listened for the sound of the car's engine behind me, hoping my hard-headed wife would do as I asked, and finally I heard it crank and heard the familiar sound of tires on the gravel drive, heading toward the road.

I didn't go through the front door, but went around the side of the house, trying to be quiet about it, though I figured that wasn't necessary. If he was in there, he had heard us drive up and probably knew I had stayed and sent them away.

I knelt down and dug out of the sand an old two-by-four that had been there for the longest time, since the carpenters expanded our garage, and tested its strength against my palm. It was still solid enough to crack a skull. I moved around to the rear of the house, expecting any moment that the bastard would jump me. I wondered what in hell I was doing, and why I hadn't gone with Ann and Jordan, but in truth I knew the answer to that. The sonofabitch had me mad and there was too much macho Texas culture in my blood in spite of myself. The sonofabitch had offended me and my family and I wanted to get hold of him and use the board on his head until my arm got tired and I had to switch to the other hand.

A part of me knew there wasn't much point to what I was doing. It was stupid. Russel had already proved he could handle me, and I didn't imagine the board amounted to much in my favor. He might even have a gun, like his son.

When I got around back I was going to use the key, but the door was open here too. The grill and the alarm hadn't done a damn thing to stop him.

I cocked the board back and stepped inside. The air-conditioning hit me like a blue norther, and the sunlight had been so harsh outside, my vision was affected. Standing there, half-blind, I felt as if I had put my balls in a vise and was waiting for someone to turn the crank.

But nothing happened. My eyes adjusted and I saw the living

room was empty and so was what I could see of the kitchen. I checked out the rest of the kitchen and went out in the enclosed garage and found the shotgun. I had remembered wrong. It was put together. The shells were with it. I loaded it and went looking through the rest of the house. I looked Jordan's room over extra hard. No one was under the bed or in the closet or hiding behind a Mickey Mouse curtain.

I tried the hall bathroom, half expecting, half hoping, Russel would come out from behind the shower curtain after me. I wanted an excuse to kill him. It wasn't that I had acquired a taste for blood, but right then I was a little crazy and I just wanted to end things between him and me, and I wanted the end to be final.

Using the barrel of the shotgun, I swept the curtain back, but he wasn't waiting for me in the tub. I went on into the master bedroom.

On the bed was the shoe box that had been in the closet and had held the gun the night of the burglary. Price still had the gun, but there had been some shells in the box, and they had been poured onto the bed and the shoe box had been ripped to shreds.

Jordan's favorite teddy bear lay there among the pieces.

13.

"It doesn't take a fucking mental giant to know he's been here," I said.

We were in the kitchen, at the table. The police had escorted Ann and Jordan home. Jordan was in the living room watching a *Casper the Friendly Ghost* videotape, and the uniform cops and detectives were going over the house like starving mice looking for crumbs. So far all they had was a torn shoe box and some .38 shells he might have touched. But I doubted he'd been that stupid. The guy was a pro. You could tell that from the way he'd handled the locks and alarms.

"We know someone has been here," Price said. "We don't know it was Russel."

Ann looked at Price. "Are you for real? I guess it was Goldilocks. There's a bear and a bed involved and if you guys can find a broken chair and some spilled porridge, you can wrap this case right up."

"Price," I said, "you know as well as I do that it was Russel. He found that shoe box with the cartridges and the gun oil stain and he put two and two together. He tore that box up and put Jordan's teddy bear on our bed as a threat. He was just showing us he can get in and get to Jordan anytime he wants."

"You're right, I think it's Russel, but I can't prove it. Since I do suspect him, we can have tabs put on him and we can watch your house. I can get official protection without any problem now. But he may be too clever for anything that obvious and we might be able to surprise him."

"Are you suggesting something?"

"We could put some obvious protection around the house for a couple of days, then pretend to be satisfied that things are normal and withdraw it—or seem to. Your son would have to start back to school then, and you and Mrs. Dane would have to return to work. Then, when he makes his move, we'll be waiting."

I looked at Ann. She got up and went over to the kitchen sink and looked out the window. I followed and put my arm around her waist.

"What do we do, Ann?"

She continued to look out the window. Finally she said, "Let's nail the bastard."

14.

The uniform cop they left with us was built like an industrial water heater and was a decorated Vietnam vet and a black belt in jujitsu. He was ugly too. I don't know why, but that kisser of his made me feel better. He didn't look like the sort to worry about his native good looks if it came down to serious business, and I figured it would take someone like him to handle Russel—even if Russel was in the ballpark of sixty years or so.

The cop's name was Kevin and they put him in a chair in the hallway, then the rest of them went outside to make their watch. The plan was simple. They would do this obvious watch for a couple of days. Not laying in the yard or anything, but staying in the woods behind the house, and patrolling regularly, posting a man in the ditch that ran to the far right of our property. They would not be overly sloppy about it, but they'd do things in such a way that if an old pro like Russel were around, he'd spot them. Then, when the couple of days were passed, they would leave. Except Kevin. He would remain in the house, having never revealed himself to the outside; he would remain and wait. Close surveillance would be maintained where we worked and where Jordan went to school. Police officers in unmarked cars would be waiting to follow us in the mornings at a safe distance and in the afternoons when we returned. Weekends, police would be hidden in the woods surrounding the house, only this time with the intent of not being seen. "Very organized, and very safe," Price said.

So we started that night. The police went away except for the few who were supposed to be in the woods behind the house and the man in the ditch. Inside, we turned on the alarms and pulled the grills in place. Considering how easily Russel had gone through them before, I felt almost silly bothering with them.

The cop had food and a coffee thermos next to his chair in the hallway. Except to go to the bathroom, he didn't plan to move. In fact, he didn't look like he could be moved; he looked as solid as a stone gargoyle.

Price called about ten. They hadn't seen Russel, but they had found his car. It was not far from our house, parked on a little dirt road that wound into the woods and ended at a dead end of trees and garbage that some of our less environmentally conscious citizens had tossed out. It seemed likely that Russel was somewhere in the area. Maybe creeping up on the house at the very moment. If Russel saw the cops and went away, more cops would be waiting at his car. If he abandoned the car, we still had our old plan. Wait a few days, make things look easy for him, then surprise him. We just had all kinds of plans.

I didn't think I'd be able to sleep, but I was more tired than I thought; worry had gnawed me down. As I was drifting off, I tried once again to imagine Russel with little Freddy, but nothing came of it. I thought then of my own father, Herman Dane. I missed him. I didn't know exactly why. He had never spent much time with me. He went hunting and fishing a lot and took me only once. He worked the rest of the time just to put food on the table. My mother called him names at night when I was supposed to be asleep. I think he loved me, but he always looked at me with a kind of astonishment, as if I had been landed in his house by aliens. I've been told I look just like him.

When I was twelve he took his beautiful Winchester rifle from the closet and loaded it in his station wagon with his rods and reels, and said he was going on a fishing trip. He let me walk him out to the car. He got down on one knee and told me he loved me and held me. That's the only time I remember such a thing. He drove away and I never saw him again. They found him in a fishing camp with the Winchester barrel in his mouth, his naked toe on the trigger. The top of his head was gone. There was talk of too many bills and another man my mother loved. I never knew for sure. I didn't go to the funeral.

My Uncle Ned, dad's brother, used to say, "He was a man of honor and integrity." I didn't understand what he meant then, but as I grew older and heard more about my dad from others, I came to understand what my Uncle Ned meant. He lived by his word and had a simple code of justice. I suppose it could have been called a Hemingway code, or some such thing. He didn't bother people and he didn't allow himself to be bothered. He stood up for himself and didn't expect others to do it. And I guess he shot himself because my mother's infidelity was just too much. Maybe being an honorable man living in a dishonorable situation was more than he could stand.

After the suicide, my mother went into a blue funk and went away, leaving me to live with my grandfather and grandmother. Two years later we heard she had died in what was then called a tourist court just outside of Amarillo. Too many pills and too many men. I didn't know how to feel about her.

But I never stopped thinking about my dad. The big hands (like Russel's) holding me, hugging me. The smell of King Edward cigars on his breath as he told me he loved me. The hollow tubes of his eyes.

I doubt I really remember his eyes. That may be a thing I've created to remember. An extra frame slipped into the motion picture of my past. But his eyes must have been that way when he left that day. My mother was a beautiful woman.

I thought of the baby Ann and I had lost, relived that horrible scenario again. Then I thought of a few nights past when Ann's elbow brought me awake and our horror cycle had begun. I reviewed the entire incident, ended it with me standing over the dead man who was sitting on our couch, his eye gone, his blood on our painting and wall.

Finally I tumbled down into the deepest part of sleep where the unremembered dreams live, and what happened next I'm not entirely sure of. But it went something like this:

Russel was even smarter than we thought he was. Breaking into the house earlier, leaving the doors open, had been a ploy. Instead of leaving, he had found the opening in our closet that led to the crawl space above, and he had pulled himself through the trap door and up there to wait among the rafters, wiring, and insulation. Even with the central air cooling the house, he would have been steaming up there. That was where all the heat rose and became trapped. He would have been basted in his own juices, his clothes clinging to him as damp and tight and hot as a thin swathe of tar. But he lay up there, not moving, silent, waiting. The day wore on and cooled near evening, and finally, when we were asleep, he opened the sliding trap in the closet and eased himself down, gently opened the door. That would have put him in a position to look right at Ann and me, helpless while we slept. But it wasn't us he wanted.

He stepped out of the closet and went to the bedroom door, closed this night due to our visitor in the hall, and he cracked it open. Our cop, thinking it was either Ann or me said, "Mr. Dane?"

I heard that down there in the deep part of sleep, and loaded with fear as I was, I came out of that sleep quickly, like a Polaris missile pushing up from the depths of the sea, breaking the waves and nosing the air.

But already Russel had jumped our cop, and there was a yell

from Kevin and the sound of something slamming against the wall in the hall, and I was rolling out of bed, grabbing at the shotgun under it, rushing for the bedroom door.

I got out in the hall just in time to see our Vietnam vet, black belt policeman take a marvelous left hook on the chin that bounced him over his chair even as his hand was in mid-draw for his revolver. The sound of the punch and the way Kevin went down like a broken manikin told me he wouldn't be getting up for a while.

It was me and Russel. He turned just as I put the shotgun on him and tried to pull the trigger, but found it was on safety. As I thumbed at the switch, Russel moved across the hall and knocked up the barrel of the gun, and as it was in action now, and my finger was firm against the trigger, it went off and a shot went into the ceiling, raining plaster on us like snow.

Through no great technique of my own, I went back and my feet got tangled with Russel's and we fell halfway into the bedroom. The shotgun went sliding away, under the bed, I think, and Russel didn't pursue it. He hit me a hard right on the forehead and my mind filled with blackness and glitter.

When the glitter fell away, I came awake to Ann yelling, "He's in Jordan's room!" And we were both up and running, me wobbling as I went.

I heard Jordan yell, "Daddy," and a weakness went through me like the worst disease you can imagine. I felt like the slowest, stupidest, most mortal person on earth. I had allowed Russel to hornswoggle me, whip me, and now he had my son.

I must have been out only fractions of a second, because by the time I got up and wobbled after Russel, he had only made it halfway to Jordan's bed, and I could see Jordan sitting up with his back against the headboard, looking at Russel.

I leaped on Russel's back and landed with my legs wrapped around his waist and my arms around his throat. He stumbled, then ran back, smashing me against the wall so violently I felt as if my spine were being pushed out through my chest. The breath went out of me and my legs and arms wouldn't hold and I let go of him and slid down the wall like a dying slug.

But now Ann was on him, almost in the daddy position I had occupied, and she was clawing at his face, and he was spinning in pain, trying to toss her off, but it was like trying to fling off a sheet wet with glue.

Finally he reached over his shoulder and got hold of her hair and jerked and bent forward at the same time and she slammed against the wall next to me and crumpled in a twist of arms and legs.

I tried to get up, but there was nothing left in me. It was as if someone had opened up a valve and let the life out of me. My breath wouldn't come. I couldn't even gasp; my lungs were jammed between a breath and an outburst. The room tilted. Russel reached the bed and Jordan screamed "Daddy" again. Russel grabbed Jordan by his pajama shirt, and with his other hand he produced from his back pocket a black shape that with a flick of his wrist sprouted a blade like a beetle showing a silver wing.

My breath came and I coiled my legs beneath me and I was moving. But I knew I was too late. Nothing could stop the thrust of that knife.

Except Russel. He froze with Jordan's pajama shirt bunched in one huge fist, the knife poised in the other like a scorpion's stinger. "Damn," he screamed, and he threw the knife hard into the headboard of the bed and let go of Jordan and I hit him like a hammer securing a nail, threw my shoulder against him and we both went flying across the room. He got his hands around my neck and stood up and my feet dangled off the floor. I tried to kick as I hung there, but I couldn't get any power in my kicks; my legs slapped at him like wet noodles.

He shoved me against the bed and kicked me in the groin and it felt as if my balls were in my ears. Then he had me on the floor, his thumbs locking behind my windpipe, and he was slamming my head against the carpet yelling, "I couldn't do it, you sonofa-bitch, couldn't do it you goddamn murdering bastard." He let go of me with one hand, and still pinning me to the floor with the other, he rained knuckles on my head. In the dim light from the hallway his teeth looked like jammed machinery gears and there were tears in his eyes big as pearls and they fell on my face hot as fresh asphalt. His blows became weaker and weaker and he kept repeating breathlessly, "you sonofabitch," and I struggled uselessly against him, flailing my fists at his side, and then Ann hit him with Jordan's Little Sprout lamp and he collapsed on top of me.

Ann stood over me, looking like a Valkyrie in her nightgown, holding a lamp in place of a sword. She looked as if she badly wanted to hit Russel again.

At first I thought my head was ringing, but it was the world coming back into focus, sight and sound. It was the alarm. The police had set it off. I could hear them wrecking the front door. They had most likely been after it ever since the shotgun had gone off. The entire battle with Russel, though it seemed longer, had taken only a few minutes.

I rolled out from beneath Russel, and Jordan ran to me. I hugged and kissed him. "It's okay," I said. "Go to your mother."

Jordan grabbed her leg and held her tight and Ann kept the lamp cocked, ready to bash Russel should he so much as fart.

I went to the front just as the police tossed aside the door and were about to shoot a riot gun into the lock on the grill.

"It's all right," I said. "He's down," and thought, bless his black heart, he couldn't do it. I got the key to the alarm and the grill-work and let the police in. They handcuffed Russel and he came to enough for them to walk him out. As he passed me, he turned and said, "I think I knew all along I couldn't do it."

"That's a big comfort to them," Price said. "Let's go." Two po-licemen took Russel out to a cop car that had appeared seemingly out of nowhere, and they drove him away.

Price and another officer got Kevin awake and onto the couch to look him over.

"You need to work on your stepover toe-hold," the officer told him.

"That old bastard is as strong as God," Kevin said.

An ambulance was called out, and a doctor came and looked at Kevin and me and my family. He clucked some, applied a bandage or two and gave us an aspirin. A cop took the knife from Jordan's headboard and Price said he'd see the front door got nailed up for the night somehow, and that tomorrow morning early he'd send a carpenter out to fix it, at the city's expense. He shook my hand and went away. Someone put the door up and there was some banging and I went over and sat on the couch with Ann and Jordan, put my arms around them, and as if by secret signal, the three of us began to cry.

15.

That night Jordan went back to bed with us and I lay there thinking about Russel. After all that had happened, the thing that kept coming back to me was that he had hands like my father and he had had them around my neck. It was like my old man had come back from the grave to choke me for something I had done. I could never quite get it out of my mind—in spite of what I knew about my mother—that I had been in some way responsible for him eating the barrel of his Winchester.

I eventually gave up trying to sleep and went into the kitchen and put some strong coffee on. While that was brewing I went into Jordan's room and turned on the light and looked around. The Little Sprout lamp, which had been beside his bed on the nightstand before Ann used it to hit Russel, lay on the floor where she had dropped it when the cops came in. There was a mark in the headboard of the bed where Russel had thrown the knife, but other than that, everything looked normal.

I walked around the room touching toys and books, assuring myself that things were as they had been and that they would coast along properly from here on out. It was a lie I very much wanted to believe.

I put the lamp where it belonged and sat down on Jordan's bed, and while I was sitting there, I saw something dark sticking out from beneath Jordan's battered toy box. Getting down on my hands and knees, I pulled it out and saw that it was a wallet. Without opening it, I knew it was Russel's and that it had slid under there during the fight.

The thing to do was to give it to the cops, but I couldn't resist a peek inside first. The first thing I saw was a photograph encased in one of those plastic windows. Russel was a young man in the picture and he looked handsome, strong and happy. He was down on his knee and he had his arm around a little blond-haired boy holding a BB gun. The boy looked about Jordan's age. On the back of the photograph was written: *Freddy and Dad.*

There was a photograph behind that one, and it was of a young man in his early twenties. He was blond, blue-eyed, and handsome, if slightly thick in the chin. On the back of the photograph in the same handwriting was *Freddy*.

I thought about Freddy the night I shot him, and tried to match his face with this one. The burglar had had brown hair sticking out from beneath his cap and the eye that wasn't a wound had been brown. His chin had been narrow, and never in his life had he been handsome or even passably attractive.

If this was a photograph of Freddy Russel, then the man I shot wasn't him.

PART TWO
FATHERS

16.

I went to the bedroom and found some clothes in the dark and managed to get out of my pajamas and put them on without waking Ann or Jordan. In the kitchen I wrote Ann a note, then slipped out quietly and drove to town.

When I got to the police station I sat in the lot for a time and leaned on the steering wheel, trying to decide if I was making a mistake. I got Russel's wallet out of my shirt pocket and opened the car door so I'd have the overhead light and looked at the photographs again and the writing on the backs of each. I must have looked at those wrinkled photographs a dozen times each, but no matter how I turned them or held them to the light, the face of the burglar I had killed was not to be found in them.

I put the wallet in the glove box of my car and got out.

Inside the station I told the dispatcher that I had come to see Price.

"He's home, sir," she said. "I can take a message."

"I think you better call him at home," I said. Then I told her who I was and what had happened and that something very important had come up. I told her I wouldn't tell anyone about it but Price, and it was something he would want to know.

"Very well," she said, and she called him, frowning at me all the while she was doing it. I found a chair and sat down and a few moments later she leaned her head out of the dispatcher's office and called to me. "He'll be here in a few minutes. He said for you to go to the assembly room and have a cup of coffee if you like."

"Thanks," I said.

"Certainly," she said, but she didn't look like she meant it.

I went back through the door that led down the hallway to the assembly room and found the coffee machine. I didn't really want the coffee, but it was something to do. I thought about backing out more than once, but that didn't happen. I just sat there with my paper coffee cup warming my hands, staring off into space.

Two cops came in laughing and looked at me in that suspicious way they look at everyone. They got coffee and sat down at the far end of the table and talked quietly and looked at me and finally got up and went out, taking their coffee with them.

I was about finished with my coffee when Price showed up. As usual, he looked perfect. He looked as if he had already had a good night's rest. His face was unlined and his black hair was combed neatly. His suit was tan and very fashionable. He had on a light blue shirt and a thin blue and tan tie and the shoes still had that blinding shoe shine.

"Problem?" he said.

"Sort of. I want you to let Russel go."

He stared at me a moment, then went over to the coffee machine and got a cup and came to sit down near me. "Why?" he said.

"He didn't really hurt anyone. He couldn't kill my son, he just thought he could."

He gave me the kind of smile nut ward attendants reserve for their patients who think they can fly. "He hurt an officer of mine. He hurt you. That wasn't exactly a tumbling act you folks were doing in there before we came in."

"No. He was trying to hurt me, all right, but he was out of his head. He wouldn't do it again. He's spent. He's had his shot and he couldn't do it and he didn't want to do it."

"So you're saying you don't want to press charges?"

"I am."

"It doesn't work like that, Mr. Dane. You don't have to press charges. We caught him in the act. He hurt one of my men. We don't need for you to press charges."

"I think you do."

"It would make it easier if you did, but we don't need you."

"The officer was hurt because he was in my house at your request."

"And at your agreement."

"Yes, but I was wrong about that."

"Come on, what's with you, Dane? Just a few hours ago you were wrestling this nut around your house, and just before that you were giving me hell for not going after him before he even tried anything."

"I know."

"Then what gives?"

I thought about the photographs in the glove box of my car, but I didn't say anything. Not yet. Something was going on here, and I was sure Price knew what it was. Or at least the department knew. And I wasn't ready to play my hole cards. I had to put Price to the test.

"I'll bring a lawyer in on this if I have to. I don't want to press charges. I want to forgive and forget, and I have a feeling Russel does too."

"Forgive and forget," Price said. "That's cute."

"It's what I want."

"I feel sorry for you," Price said. "One moment you're a fucking Nazi right-winger wanting me to get this bastard off your ass, and now you're a bleeding-heart liberal leaking blood all over the goddamn floor. You're schizo. You don't know what you're asking.

This man is dangerous. He tried to kill your son because you had to kill his. He tried to kill you and your wife and he injured one of my men. If I were you, I wouldn't take that lightly. I'd leave the turn-the-other-cheek stuff to the Sunday school lessons and the five-year-olds. We're living in the real world here, Dane, and Jesus wouldn't last five fucking minutes in it. No one would bother to crucify his passive ass. Takes too long. They'd run him over with a car or cut his guts out with a rusty can opener."

"I don't need a lecture."

"You need something, Dane. Hell, man, you can't be serious. Think about what you're asking."

"I've been thinking about it. I want Russel let go. I don't want to press charges, and if I don't get what I want, I'm going to bring a lawyer in on this. I promise you that. I want him out now, where I can see him set free, and I want charges dropped. I just want to get on with my life and let him get on with his."

"You really think I can do that?"

"I think you better."

He sat and looked at me and tore his empty coffee cup apart and then tore it into smaller pieces. Finished, he put both hands on the table and kept his eyes on me.

"Don't try and scare me, Price, it just makes me tired."

"I pity you."

"You said that. Now either let Russel out, or I call my lawyer and you folks start having problems."

It was my turn to stare this time, and I gave it all I had. After a moment he stood up, raked the destroyed paper cup into one hand, went over to the trash can and deposited it.

"You're making a big mistake, Dane. But it's your life. And your family's. I may not be there to pull your ass out of the fire next time."

"As I recall, Ann and I did the pulling. Your man was on the floor."

He gave me a look that made his handsome face ugly.

"You got it, buddy. I'll let him out. Just remember when he comes after you, I told you so."

"I'll wait out in the parking lot just to make sure he's set free."

"You dumb bastard," Price said, and left the room.

He had failed the test. It had been too easy. There was more to this than met the eye. And Price was in on it.

17.

I was in the lot leaning on the hood of my car with Russel's wallet in my pocket when he came out escorted by Price and a uniformed policeman. The three of them stood there looking at me and then Price gave Russel a slight nudge with his hand and Russel walked over toward me. Price and the uniform stayed where they were.

When Russel got to me he said, "They're waiting to see if I try and kill you."

"Are you going to try?"

"No."

I waved Price and the uniform cop away.

"Leave the lot," Price yelled back. "Get killed somewhere else."

Russel turned and smiled at them. "You don't have faith in me, Lieutenant."

"You're both sick," Price said and went inside. The uniform stayed where he was.

"Get in," I said. "We have to talk."

Russel got in and I cranked the car and drove out of the lot and coasted slowly down California Street. "What do you think?" I said.

"I agree with Price. You're loony. I tried to kill you a little while ago. You know I was really trying."

"You didn't kill my son. You had the chance."

"I couldn't have.... Hell, I don't know if I could have killed you."

"You banged me around good enough."

"I thought I wanted to kill somebody. I hate your guts, you know?"

"Because I killed your son?"

Russel made a noise somewhere between a hummph and a cough.

"I didn't kill him," I said.

"Look. You're crazy enough to get me out of jail.... I don't know how, but you did, but don't be so crazy as to think I'm gonna believe that shit. Just let me off somewhere, all right?"

"Let me show you something." I fished the wallet out of my shirt pocket and flipped it open with one hand to the photographs and handed it to him. I turned on the inside light. "That's your son, right?"

"You know damn good and well it is. If you're trying to find out if I'll kill you after all, you're on the right track."

"You're sure the boy and the man in those pictures are your son, Freddy?"

"I know my own son."

I turned off the inside light. "That's not the man I shot."

We drove on in silence until Russel said, "You mean you don't recognize him from these photographs?"

"I mean that isn't the man I shot. He couldn't have changed enough to be the man I shot. How tall is Freddy?"

"I don't know. Tall. Tall as me."

"At least six foot?"

"Yeah. I haven't seen him in a while. We haven't been in contact. He could have changed a lot."

"Could his eyes have changed from blue to brown?"

"Contacts maybe."

"No. This man wasn't wearing contacts. He was also shorter, darker. It wasn't your son."

"What in hell are you saying, Dane?"

"I'm saying something screwy is going on."

Russel thought for a while and I turned right on Crane Street and hit the main drag and turned left. "Why should I believe you?" he said. "Maybe you're just jerking me around. I'm told by the cops my son is dead and I find out you did it, and now you want me to believe different just because you say so."

"What's in this for me?" I said. "Think about it. You damn near beat my head in earlier and you threatened my son. Not something I'll forget or forgive you for, even if I do believe you couldn't have done it. Hell, I could be wrong. You could kill me and my whole family and it would be my fault. But I didn't kill your son. I knew that when I saw the photographs. I don't know who I killed or why the police said he was Freddy Russel, but I'm convinced it wasn't a mistake on their part. They did what they did on purpose. If they hadn't, they wouldn't have let you out no matter how many lawyers I threatened. They let you out because they were afraid I'd raise a stink and reveal something else. Something they're trying to hide about your son."

Another pregnant silence before, "So what if I believe you? What do I do?"

"What do *we* do," I said. "I'm in this too."

We went to an All-Night Doughnut Shop on North Street. It, along with a Kroger store, are about it beyond ten at night and before six or seven in the morning. They stay open for the college kids.

The All-Night Doughnut Shop had a couple of young guys at a table drinking coffee, looking over books, probably cramming for a test that they should have been studying for for a month. A somewhat older guy was behind the doughnut counter and he looked like he'd been there all night and was ready for a fresh recruit. When I ordered a couple of doughnuts and coffees for us, he didn't say any more than he had to, like maybe his mouth was tired.

We took a table at the rear of the place and after sipping at our coffee, Russel said, "I still don't see why you're bothering. What do you care about me?"

I slid sideways in the booth so I could put my feet along the seat and my back against the wall and not have to look directly at Russel. "Personally, I don't give a shit about you. I don't even like you. Why should I?"

"Why then? You could have just let things slide."

"I've been hoodwinked. I don't like that. I killed a man and I don't even know who I killed. I don't like that. Because they said I killed your son it made you crazy enough to threaten my son and try to hurt me and my wife. I don't like that. But I'm a human being. I think I know some of how you must have felt, your son dead and all. I think I'd have been a little crazy. I'm not forgiving you, mind you, I'm just saying I've got some idea about how you must have felt, and then for it all to be a lie...."

"I never did that boy any real good when he was alive," Russel said. "I'm not sure why I thought I could do him any now. Guilt maybe."

"You see him much?"

"No. Just when he was younger. Those pictures were about it. His mom may have made him send the one where he was older. I don't know. That was years back. Me and his mom were separated, but she still kept in touch, let me know how Freddy was doing. The football team, stuff like that."

"What were you in for?"

"Burglary at first. I got out and then I went back in on an armed robbery charge. I got off light because it couldn't be proved I had the gun. Which I didn't. The guy with me had the gun."

"Same difference, isn't it?"

"Just about. I kept him from killing the store attendant. He shot the attendant once and I hit him and wrestled the gun away. It wasn't supposed to be like that, the shooting I mean. I just needed money and we were going to bluff. Or so he said. I didn't know the asshole was a cold killer."

"So they got you while you were fighting with your partner?"

"No. I took the gun from him and coldcocked him and waited until they called the law. I figured things were bad enough with the store manager bleeding to death without me making it worse for myself by running. And the truth is, had I left my partner, he'd have talked. I didn't want to kill him, so I stayed and took my medicine. One of the clerks testified that I had stopped my partner from finishing the man off, but it didn't matter really. He died later."

"What happened to your partner?"

"He was one of the last to get the chair—this was before the injection stuff. I got a stretch."

"What plans did you have when you got out...before this thing happened with your son? Or the man who was supposed to be your son?"

"I sat in there twenty years trying to figure out what I wanted to do. Some things crossed my mind. Wasn't any of them any good. I wanted to find my son and make up for lost time. That was about it. I'd have taken any kind of job just so I could be near him, or go to see him from time to time. I had a lot of catching up to do. Some explaining. But that's all shit under the bridge now."

"Your son is probably out there somewhere, we just have to figure how to find him."

Russel laid those hands that looked like my father's hands on the table and looked at them, as if trying to determine how they had gotten there on the ends of his wrists. Finally he lifted his head. "There was this guy I knew once. We were good friends before I got stupid. He was a character. But hell, I haven't seen him in twenty years. He'd be about fifty now, I think. He wrote me in jail some and I wrote back for a while, then quit. His letters kept coming. He knew me and my family, you see."

"What about him?"

"He was a private investigator. Real good. I worked for him some doing skip traces and repossessions before I got stupid. He had quite a reputation."

"Where is he?"

"I don't know now. He was in Houston then. He'd been in the military. A Green Beret. Expert in all that Jap fighting. He taught me some. Good boxer too. Knew about guns. Name is Jim Bob Luke."

"You think he could help us find some things out?"

"If he's still out there and will do it, yeah. If he can't, no one can."

I thought about that a while. In spite of my humanity speech I was beginning to feel like a jackass. I had gotten Russel out of jail and that was enough. Like he said, I didn't owe that to him. Maybe he was crazy and maybe he didn't believe a word I was saying. He was just waiting for a chance to finish what he started. And what would Ann think about all this? Not only had I gotten him out of the slammer, I was now planning to help him find out what happened to his son. Hire some private detective to do it. It didn't make much sense.

But then again I thought about the man I had killed. You didn't just kill a man and not know his name. And I didn't like the idea of being used. I wasn't sure how the police had used me, but they had. And this poor bastard might never have gone off his head for even a little bit had they not told him the lie they did. And it seemed like the more I tried to rationalize not getting involved any more than I already was, the more I felt I should.

"A detective costs money," Russel said, voicing my next concern. "I don't have any, and I don't think Jim Bob will do it for free. Maybe he would have in the old days, but I don't know now. Lot of time has gone by. I feel like it was yesterday that we were friends, but my contacts have been kind of limited the last few years. Jim Bob has probably gone on and had a life. He may not want anything to do with me—even if I had money to hire him."

"I can supply the money," I said. "I'm not made of it, but I do all right. First thing, let's see if he's still around."

I drank my coffee and went outside to the phone booth between the doughnut shop and the Fina station and called Houston information. I asked first for a Luke Detective Agency, then for a Jim Bob Luke. Neither was listed.

I tried Pasadena, which is a small burg outside of Houston. A lot of people drive to work in Houston from there.

"Jim Bob Luke on Mulberry Street?" the operator asked.

I took a flyer. "Yeah, that's him."

She gave me the number and I wrote it on one of my business cards and went back to the doughnut shop. I slid into the booth across from Russel and said, "Bingo."

18.

There was a lightening of the sky by the time we left the doughnut shop. I drove Russel to the Lazy Lodge on the edge of town and checked him in for the day. It's a sleazy place that caters to the wetbacks passing through on their way to shitty jobs and enough money to rent a mobile home for twelve. Meals were served from a candy and soft drink machine in the grungy lobby. For a dollar or so you could have a Snickers and a Coke.

I gave Russel enough money for emergencies, like Coke and Snickers and a throw-away razor of the sort they sold at the check-in desk.

"You taking me in to raise?" Russel said.

"Seems like it," I said.

We went into the little room he was assigned and left the door half open as it was hot in there and the air-conditioning wasn't turned on. The room had the faint smell of an uncleaned toilet and too much lemon air freshener. Three dead roaches had been piled in one corner on top of one another by an indifferent broom stroke, making them look like an insect balancing act.

Russel sat on the bed and it sagged so bad in the middle he seemed to be melting from the butt up. He worked his way out of the slump and got down on his knees and looked under the bed and laughed. "Only one slat in the middle. Swank."

"It's all my finances will allow," I said.

"I'm not complaining." He sat on the very edge of the bed and got out his cigarette pack and shook out the last cigarette and put it in his mouth. He didn't light it, just let it dangle there. "You really going to help me find my son?"

"Yeah."

"You trust me after what I did?"

"I don't know. I must. Either that or I'm crazy."

"It was a kind of calculated madness, Dane. I thought I knew what I wanted to do, but I couldn't do it. It seemed sane to me when I first thought it. A son for a son, but I knew inside me I couldn't do it. But I could have killed you.... I've thought about it all morning. I told you in the car I didn't know if I could have. That was a lie. I could have. I thought you killed my son and it wouldn't have been anything for me to do you in."

"You'd have gone back to prison."

"Big shit. I'd have been just as happy if they'd killed me."

"And now?"

"I don't know. If my son's alive I want to find him. It makes all the difference in the world."

I had been standing. I found the only chair in the room and sat down on it. It groaned as if in pain.

"They don't hold back on expense here, do they?" Russel said.

"Was your cell any better?" I was feeling mean. I still didn't like the sonofabitch and he had just admitted that he could have killed me and slept.

But my question didn't bother him. He actually considered it.

"The only thing that made the cell bad was that the door was closed and I couldn't open it anytime I wanted. But out here, I'm like a duck out of water. I've been away from civilian life too long. I don't know how to act. Don't even know how to talk to a woman anymore. I'm not sure which is worse. Here or Huntsville."

"Sad how they make you serve your time, isn't it?"

He smiled at me. "I deserved my time, Dane. I'm not complaining." He found a match then and lit his cigarette. "Last smoke and last match."

"I gave you enough money for cigarettes and food. I'll get back in touch with you."

"You're going to contact Jim Bob?"

"Yeah."

"It may not be the same one, you know?"

"I know, but with a name like Jim Bob Luke, I figure it is. I'd more likely think he might not be in the same business."

"Maybe you could let me talk to him. We used to be friends."

"So you've said. Maybe that's enough reason for me to leave that sucker alone."

"He's wiser than me," Russel said. "He believes in justice and truth and liberty and all that shit."

"All right, you talk to him. They've got a pay phone here. When you've gotten some rest and you think he might be up, call him."

Daybreak was edging in the open doorway and that made me think of Ann and Jordan. "I have to go home," I said.

"When will I hear from you?"

"I don't know. I've got some thinking to do. You get something from Jim Bob Luke, you call me. My number's in the book."

I stood up.

"Dane, an apology isn't much after what I did—"

"No, it isn't."

"But I'm offering it."

"Wouldn't have done me much good if you'd have killed me and my family."

"I wouldn't have killed your family. Just you."

"That makes me feel a sight better, Russel."

"Put yourself in my situation and think about what you'd have done."

"I wouldn't have done what you did."

"That wasn't much thought on the matter."

"I know I wouldn't have done what you did."

"No, I don't think you would have either. I'm not offering an excuse, just an apology."

"Your apology is shit, Russel."

"We're going to have to work together on this. Me finding my son and you finding out who you killed, what this is all about. We might as well get along and learn to trust one another."

"I don't know if I can trust you completely, Russel. I'm already having my doubts and thinking I should have left you where you were. Maybe you don't deserve a son."

"I can't argue with that."

I didn't like the way this was going. "Just lay low. You get in trouble and you're on your own. I can't help you anymore, and I wouldn't if I could."

"We're going to be helping each other plenty if we get into this. If the cops are in on it like you say, they aren't going to hand us the answers on a platter."

"Rest. I'll see you later."

I stopped off at the phone booth between the Fina and the doughnut shop and called home and didn't explain much, just said I'd be there shortly and I wasn't going to work today. After that I called Valerie and told her I wouldn't be in and to take her key.

When I finished talking and started driving home, I thought about what I had done and I wondered how I was going to explain it to Ann. I wasn't sure I could explain it to myself. Russel was an ex-con and he wasn't any saint and he didn't need a son. He needed a nice warm cell and someone to feed him and tell him when to bathe and when to shit and when to breathe. Why did I want to bother with him anyway? What could possibly come of this? Even if I found out who I killed, how would that change things? A dead Wilbur Smith is no better than a dead John Doe. The earth would not shift on its axis either way.

COLD IN JULY

So how did I explain? What could I tell Ann that would make her understand? Should I say that Russel had hands like my father?

19.

When I came in Ann was fixing toast.

"You want some?"

"No. I had a doughnut in town. I'll have some coffee with you, though."

"What was with the note? Where have you been?"

"Where's Jordan?" I asked.

"Asleep still. I thought I'd let him skip day school today. I called in at work. I'm not going either. What about my question?"

"I went to the police station."

She considered that a moment. "About getting the door fixed?"

"No. I went to talk to them about Russel."

"Yeah?"

"I asked them to let him go."

She was busy putting her toast on the plate and now she turned to look at me. "Letting him go?"

"I found a wallet in Jordan's bedroom. Russel's. It had a picture of his son in it. It wasn't the man I shot."

"You asked the police to let that bastard go after what he did?"

"There wasn't any way it was Freddy Russel. This guy didn't look anything like him. The man I shot wasn't Freddy Russel. I went and asked them to let him go and they did."

Her knees went weak and she dropped the plate and the toast. The plate broke and the toast went sliding under the table. She leaned her back against the counter and I went over there to help her.

"Stay where you are," she said. "Don't touch me."

"Listen, I spent all morning with Russel."

"God, they really let him out?"

"He wants to find out the same things I do. Who it was I shot and why they said it was his son and where his son is. We're going to hire a private detective out of Houston."

"Richard, you've gone nuts. That man tried to kill Jordan."

"He couldn't do it."

"He tried to kill you. If I hadn't hit him with that goddamn lamp he would have."

"Maybe," I said. "I don't think so. He was a little crazy is all."

"And now he's cured?"

"I spent all morning with him and he didn't try a thing. He talked sensibly. I think he can be trusted. I put him up in a motel."

Ann went over to the table and pulled out a chair and sat down. "You did what?"

"I put him up in a motel. I'm supposed to call him later."

"Why don't you invite him for supper, you dumb shit? Invite him over. Ask him what he wants to eat, ask him what his favorite is. When he's finished dinner he can take me in the bedroom and fuck me then kill you and Jordan. Maybe then he might like to set the house on fire. We've got plenty of matches and we could always buy some kerosene. Have it on hand."

"Ann, you're not being reasonable."

"I'm not? Godalmighty, Richard. What in the world has gotten into you? You've flipped that little pea brain of yours."

"Don't talk so loud, you'll wake Jordan up."

"I'll talk any goddamn way I want to.... God, Jesus Christ, Richard.... They let him out?"

"That's why I know the police were in on this. Hiding the burglar's identity. Giving him Freddy Russel's name. Think about it. They wouldn't have let him out that easy, they just wouldn't. They didn't want me to bring in a lawyer and get the whole thing in court and bring some things out they didn't want to talk about."

She hadn't been looking at me, but now she turned her lovely green eyes on me and stared, didn't say a word, just stared. I felt like I should start braying.

"I can't believe you," she said. "I just can't." Then she got up and left the room.

I poured myself a cup of coffee and sat at the table and looked at the coffee, and after a while I got up and poured it in the sink and cleaned up the toast and broken dish. I went into the living room and stretched out on our new couch, and I was more exhausted than I thought. I fell asleep immediately, only to be awakened by a soft movement on my forehead.

I opened my eyes and Ann was on her knees next to the couch leaning over me. Her blond hair was falling down her face and onto mine and I could see the fine crow's feet that had just begun to form at the edge of her magnificent eyes and they looked just fine to me. She had her hand on my forehead, and she was pushing my hair back. "You're right," she said. "They wouldn't have let him go that easy. There's something going on. I think what you did was stupid and you should have talked to me first, but you're right, them letting him go like that doesn't add up. Tell me all of it. Top to bottom."

"After I kiss you," I said.

My appetite came back and we had coffee and toast and I told her all of it again only in greater detail. I told her exactly how Russel had acted and what he had said to me, and I told her about this

Jim Bob Luke character who might be a detective Russel once knew.

"Baby," she said, "I don't want to reopen the wound, but Russel could be crazy as a loon, and even if you didn't kill his son, he may not believe you. He may be planning to get in your good graces so he can get to Jordan. I just think what you did was...stupid."

"Maybe. But he had his chance to kill Jordan and I couldn't have stopped him. He chose not to. He had his chance to kill me today, and I think had he wanted to he would have done it and damned anyone seeing him. I don't think he would have cared, because he knew the police would know he did it, since I was stupid enough to drive off with him. No, I think the man was literally out of his mind from grief, and when it came down to root hog or die, he couldn't do it. It took all the wind out of his sails. All he wants now is to find his son. I'm not saying I like the guy, I'm just saying I'm not afraid of him now."

"Okay, he's out. But what's it to you, baby? He can search for his son on his own."

"He hasn't got the money."

"That's his problem." I could see the spark coming back into her eyes and I wanted to fan it down before we went through a similar scene like the earlier one. Ann had a temper, and even when she cooled, she could flare up faster than a windblown coal.

"The money isn't just for him. He finds his son, I can find out who it was I killed."

"What's it matter?"

"I can find out why the police are doing this."

"Again, what's it matter? Jordan is safe, we're safe, and now Russel is free. Justice is served, and if there's any more to it, that's Russel's problem. It doesn't matter what the burglar's name was. He isn't anyone we'd want to know. He tried to kill you."

"It's the principle of the thing."

"Principle. Who has principles?"

"I do."

"Yeah, tough guy. The macho code."

"It's more than that. I can't look myself in the eye if I just drop it."

"So quit using mirrors."

"Shit, Ann, I can't do it. You know me better than that."

"This honor stuff has been okay up until now and kind of cute, Richard. You've railed about it before, and it was always something trivial. You told the truth when you could have lied and bettered yourself. Admirable. You stood by a friend when he was down. Nice. You had scruples. Wonderful. But it's Sunday school stuff. It's not for real life. Not when it gets big and nasty, baby."

"Price gave me a similar speech from a different angle. He didn't call me baby though."

She almost smiled at me. "This is something to do with the law. Maybe they know what they're doing. Maybe it's best we don't know."

"They could have gotten one of us killed just by lying, by saying the man I shot was Freddy Russel. If they hadn't lied in the first place, none of this would have happened. I want to know why."

"You want to make sure you don't tarnish your damn honor," she said, getting up a bit too quickly and pouring herself a fresh cup of coffee and sloshing it onto the counter.

"It's something to believe in. It makes me believe in myself, and with what faults I've got, I've got that to believe in, and it's the only thing I can pass on to my son that's worth a shit. It's all I have of my dad."

"He shot himself, Richard. His sense of honor didn't keep him from doing that. He found out your mother was cheating on him and he couldn't take it. It offended his macho pride and he blew his brains out.... Oh, Richard, I didn't mean to say that.... Not that way."

I sat silent for a moment. "I think he shot himself because he failed himself. He didn't live up to the man he thought he ought to be. I think he felt like he was taking seconds when he took his wife to bed at night and that he was learning to be satisfied with it. He knew he should have confronted her or left, or both, but he couldn't, and that was the thing he couldn't live with, being weak that way. He found it easier to go all the way out than to just walk out."

"You're guessing, Richard."

"Yeah, but I think I'm right. I can sympathize with him not feeling he was living up to who he wanted to be. I'm not saying if I don't do this thing I'll kill myself, because I won't, but I am saying, I'd like to see what I'm made of. I don't think I can come home and watch TV and read the newspapers and let this go like nothing ever happened. It would eat at my guts for the rest of my life. Aren't you in the least bit curious, Ann? Don't you want to know what's going on and why?"

She started to say no, then paused. "All right," she said. "Let's see if we can find out what it's all about."

20.

I called the Lazy Lodge. Russel sounded tired and old when he answered.

"Use some of that money I gave you to call Jim Bob Luke," I said. "I'll give you some more. Ann and I are coming there for lunch soon as we get Jordan squared away."

"Your wife?"

"I believe you know her name. You know all our names and a lot about us. Remember, you researched us?"

There was a long silence. "All right, bring her."

"I intended to. You call Jim Bob and see if it's the man you knew and if he's still doing what he used to do and if he'll work for us. We'll bring you a hamburger or something when we come. We can make plans from there."

"What's Jim Bob's number?"

I gave it to him.

"How does your wife feel about this?" Russel asked.

"She hates your guts. I'm surprised she'll even be in the same room with you."

"This is going to be cozy. Wish I could make it up to her."

"Well, you can't. Just sit tight and make the call. We'll be there before too long."

We went by Jordan's day school and checked him in late. Then we stopped off at Burger King and ate so we wouldn't have to eat with Russel. That was too damn friendly. When we finished I bought him a hamburger and french fries and a soft drink and we drove to the Lazy Lodge.

Ann looked the place over. "Looks just right for him."

We got out and walked to Russel's room. The door was still open and Russel was sitting on the bed looking at us. I went on in, but Ann stood in the doorway looking at him. Russel couldn't hold her gaze. He checked out some tatters in the rug, which looked older than original sin.

"Come in, Ann," I said.

I waved her to the chair I had sat in, and when she was seated it groaned at her the way it had at me. I gave Russel the sack with the food in it and he sat it on the bed beside him and didn't open it. "Thanks," he said.

I leaned against the wall and crossed my arms and felt the heat of the room nestle about me like chain mail. The air-conditioner still wasn't on.

"You talk to Jim Bob Luke?" I asked.

Russel stole a glance at Ann, still didn't like what he saw, so he looked at me. "Yeah."

"Well?"

"It's the same Jim Bob Luke, all right."

"For Christsake, Russel, tell me what he said."

"He's coming. He'll be here in about three hours. I told him everything. He sounds just the same. It was like it was yesterday I saw him last."

"I'm glad you talked about old times," Ann said, "but is he going to help us when he gets here?"

"He is."

"Jesus," Ann said, and she got up and walked out the door.

98

I walked out after her. She had gone about halfway down the walk and was leaning against the wall, looking across the highway like it was a raging river she had to swim.

"You okay?" I said.

"How did I let you talk me into this?"

"Ann, I'm worn down and I know you are. I'm going to do this thing and I'd like for you to see it through with me. I'm not going to argue anymore. I'm doing this because I've got to. I'd like for you to understand and accept it. At least tolerate it. We've been together for a long time for you not to trust me."

I held out my hand.

She didn't smile; but she took my hand and we walked back to Russel's room.

About two-thirty an ancient blood-red Cadillac about the size of a submarine pulled up directly in front of the door to Russel's room. There were baby shoes hanging off the mirror along with a big, yellow, foam-rubber dice, and on the windshield was a homemade sticker that had six stick-figure humans and three dogs drawn on it and there was an X through each of them. The car had curb feelers and they were still wobbling violently when the driver got out and slammed the door and stretched.

"Shit," Russel said. "That's Jim Bob's Caddy. That sucker's twenty years old. It was new when I went in the joint."

I could see the man stretching beside the door, and he looked like a washed-up country and Western singer. He was tall and lean and wore a worn straw hat with a couple of anemic feathers in it. He had on a white cowboy shirt with thin green stripes in it and faded blue jeans and boots that looked like they had often waded through water and shit.

Russel got off the bed and went out there and I heard the cowboy yell, "Goddamn, ole horse, you look like smoking dog shit."

"I been sick," Russel said pleasantly.

"Sick! You look like you been dead and some ignorant fuck dug you up. Good to see you again, you sorry asshole. How's it hanging?"

"It's hanging fine. Jim Bob, there's a lady in the room here."

"One that costs money?"

"No, a real lady."

"Shit, me and my goddamn mouth."

And then Jim Bob came into the room behind Russel and I got a real look at him. His age was hard to determine, but from what Russel had said, I knew he was at least fifty. He had a pleasant, tanned (except where his hat protected his forehead), thin face and a mouth that was full of nice, white teeth made for smiling.

"You must be Mr. Dane?" he said.

I shook hands with him and introduced Ann.

"You didn't mention a woman," Jim Bob said to Russel.

"My surprise," Russel said.

"Howdy, ma'am. I'm sorry for the way I was talking out there in the parking lot, but I didn't know a lady was in here."

"Just treat me like one of the guys," Ann said.

"No, ma'am, I couldn't do that. Only a deaf, dumb and blind fella could treat you like one of the guys. You darn sure don't look like no one of the guys."

"Thank you," Ann said after a pause.

"Man, Ben," Jim Bob said, "this place looks like a Juarez whore-house, couldn't you have done no better than this?"

"Well," Russel said, "actually, Mr. Dane paid for these accommodations."

"That right?" Jim Bob said. "I don't call this here accommodations. I've seen nigger rent shacks better than this."

"I wasn't trying to find Russel a permanent place to live," I said, "just a place to nest for a time."

"Nest?" Jim Bob said. "If you was a bird would you nest here? Hell, a bird wouldn't shit here, let alone nest.... Pardon my French, ma'am."

I looked at Ann and she looked at me. The expression on her face was noncommittal. Too noncommittal.

"Tell you what, lady and men, we're gonna shag on out of this place and get on out to the Holiday Inn. Get some good grub and maybe even one of them magic fingers beds for ole Ben here, then we'll get to shoveling our piles, all right?"

"Jim Bob," I said, "I don't even know you. Did Russel explain what's going on here?"

"Yeah, he wants to find his son and you want to find out whose brains you blew out and why the cops lied to you and what they're up to. But that don't mean we got to stand around here in this sweatbox with this good-looking lady perched on that rotten chair like a parrot. Let's go on over and get some air-conditioning. I do a lot better thinking when I have a big ole steak under my belt and a couple of cold Lone Stars to ride on top of it. I don't do my best thinking when I'm hot as a Cuban whore and the place smells like a pig's favorite corner, and I ain't knocking pigs 'cause I own a dozen of them—Yorkshires. But folks, this ain't headquarters."

Ann and I followed Jim Bob and Russel over to the Holiday Inn. The Cadillac was impossible to lose, even though the way Jim Bob drove you would have thought he was doing his best to get rid of us. But that damn Caddy stood out like a brushfire from six blocks ahead.

"That bozo's the private detective?" Ann asked.

"You were expecting Mike Hammer or Jim Rockford?"

"I was expecting someone who could read and write. That moron hasn't got the sense to get out of the rain, let alone detect. He couldn't find his ass with both hands and a road map."

I laughed.

"It isn't funny," Ann said, but she laughed a little. "He's out to get our money and Russel is along for the ride. They're both crazy, and we're crazy as they are."

"Well, Jim Bob is peculiar."

"Peculiar. He's a cracker. A redneck. A loony tune. Did you hear what he said, nigger shack. I hate that word, nigger. I despise it. This is not only crazy, the man we're in with is a bigot."

"I didn't choose their company because they're such liberated, socially conscious individuals. I didn't choose Russel at all, and Jim Bob sounded like a good idea at the time. If he's a yo-yo, I won't hire him."

"He considers himself hired, I think," Ann said. "The Holiday Inn for headquarters? He must think we'll put him up there. We don't need a headquarters, and they can sleep in that red monstrosity he drives for a car. Did you see those baby shoes and the dice? Those silly curb feelers?"

"You don't criticize the blacks and the Mexicans for their dice and baby shoes," I said, and wished I hadn't said it. She didn't speak to me all the rest of the way to the Holiday Inn.

21.

We ate at the Holiday Inn restaurant, or rather Jim Bob did. The rest of us had tea and coffee and Ann had a slice of apple pie. Jim Bob ordered steak and baked potato and all the trimmings, and when he took his first bite of steak he waved the waitress over and told her, "Honey, take this cow on back and finish killing it. Set the little buddy on fire for about three more minutes then bring it back to me."

While Jim Bob waited on the steak, he and Russel talked about old times, and laughed. Ann and I felt a little limp, as if we had gone to the wrong party.

When Jim Bob's steak came back he thanked the waitress and ordered a Lone Star Light. "Got to watch my girlish figure," and he went at his food with gusto, saying, "Brain food."

"Then you better eat plenty of it," Ann said.

I looked at her. Russel looked at her. Jim Bob looked at her, and laughed. "Ain't that the damned truth," he said. "Pass that salad dressing. The one that looks like someone threw up in the bottle."

Ann looked at him blankly and passed the dressing. Well, Jim Bob wasn't easy to insult, and I had a feeling that was because he'd had plenty of practice dodging catty remarks.

"Now, what we have here," Jim Bob said, "is a real strange situation. And whatever is going on, the cops are in on it. And I figure that new tan Ford that followed us from across the highway after we left that sleaze motel is a cop car, and the fella that parked it out in the lot and come in here when we did and is sitting over there drinking his twelfth cup of coffee and rereading the sports section for the third time is a cop. Cops and cop cars go together, as the little ole man said. Whatever you people have put your feet in, it's deep stuff."

"You don't know that's a cop," Ann said.

"No, ma'am, I don't. But I figure it is, and I figure pretty good. Wouldn't have been in this line of work long as I have if I didn't. And if you feel a little hostile to me, that's all right, sister. I don't blame you. I know Ben here, and after what he's done you're connecting me with him. We're friends, but we're separate, and what he did was a killing offense. I'd have killed him myself. But we're past that. Ben was a little crazy, but now he's right as rain, or as right as he gets. So we're gonna work together, or let's just get this over so I can take ole Ben back to Houston for a three-day drunk and see if I can get him a job somewhere. What say? We gonna work together or not?"

"I didn't say anything about any of that," Ann said.

"Well, you did and you didn't. What's it gonna be, Mr. and Mrs. Dane?"

I looked at Ann.

Ann said, "All right. The man over there is a policeman, and we'll work together."

"Good," Jim Bob said. "What we're gonna have to do first is go out there and dig up that fella you shot."

"What?" I said.

"You heard me. I want to be sure that the dead fella isn't Freddy.

I know what you've said, and I don't think you're a liar, but you could be wrong. He could have changed a lot. The color of the eyes you could have been wrong about. I've dealt with a lot of eyewitnesses, and what they remember ain't always how it was. In your case, you may not want that ole burglar to be Freddy, but it could be."

"No way," I said.

"That's the rules," Jim Bob said. "We start there. If it is Freddy, then we figure why they let Ben out so easy and take it from there. If it ain't Freddy, we play another angle. And let me add this." He looked at Russel. "If it is Freddy, and if you're still thinking you got to hurt Mr. Dane or his family here, well, Ben, ole hoss, I'll just have to blow your brains out and put you in the hole with him and cover you up. Got me?"

Russel grinned at him. "I may not let you."

"We can always hope we don't have to find that out, can't we?"

"Yeah," Russel said. "I wouldn't want to kill you, Jim Bob, we been friends too long."

"It would pain me too. Killing you or getting killed by you, so let's just hope that don't come up."

"It won't. If it's Freddy, then I'll accept he was burglarizing Dane's house and Dane had to kill him." Russel looked at me. "I know now you didn't just shoot him unarmed and plant a gun. You aren't like that."

"My, haven't we gotten to be chummy," Ann said.

"And little lady," Jim Bob said, "you keep that sarcastic edge, 'cause we're gonna need it to keep us sharp. Now, let me finish up this feast, then I'd like to get Ben and me checked into a room. Mr. and Mrs. Dane, y'all go on home and I'll call you. And if you're starting to sweat a little bit in the pocketbook and wondering what I'm gonna cost you, it's like this. Three hundred dollars a day, no expenses. I cut that 'cause I know Ben. As for the stay at the Holiday Inn for me and Ben, I got that covered. If that sounds steep to you, don't know what to tell you. That's the price. I don't just do this for my health and I ain't so friendly to Ben here I'll do it for free."

"That's all right," I said.

"It's high," Ann said.

"It'll do," I said.

Jim Bob laughed. "Don't you just love women? They can squeeze a dollar till it farts—no offense ma'am. Listen, you two go home and I'll call you when I want you. I won't give details over the phone. I'll just call and you come here and we'll talk in person. Way this is shaping up, could be something big and nasty going on here, and if that's the case, they're out at your place tapping the phones right now."

I thought about that and couldn't really imagine it. It sounded too much like one of those bad made-for-television movies.

"If the fella over there follows you out and follows you home, don't pay him no mind. It don't mean a thing. Or he might have a buddy follow you. But you just go home and wait. Got me?"

"Got you," I said.

"Lady," Jim Bob said, "you don't have to come back if you don't want to. But if you come, I want you to be cooperative, and I don't want you worrying about snagging your panty hose or such. We'll be humping right along, I figure, and we don't need no slackers."

"I assure you, Mr. Jim Bob," Ann almost whistled through her teeth, "I'm not a slacker."

"I didn't actually figure you for one," Jim Bob said.

"Jim Bob likes to ingratiate himself with his clients," Russel said. "Make 'em feel trusted and warm."

"My business ain't public relations—unless I'm lying for a good reason," Jim Bob said. "But I don't lie to my employers. It's not the way it's done."

Ann got up and started out of the hotel restaurant without saying a word. I stood and took out my wallet.

"Nah," Jim Bob said. "You folks just had pie and coffee. I'll get it and the tip. Go on and catch up with her. And, Dane, tell her she's right, three hundred a day is high. But I'm the best there is, and by God, I don't normally pay my own expenses."

On the way home Ann turned the radio on too loud and sat on the far side of the car with her arms crossed, and after a while she turned the radio off and drummed her fingers on the dash.

Jordan was in the backseat looking puzzled. Ever since we had picked him up at the day school he had known something was going on, but he didn't know exactly what.

"Mommy, you mad at Daddy?"

"Just a little," she said.

"Don't be mad at Daddy."

"It'll pass," she said.

God, I hoped so.

When we got home, we made arrangements for the Fergusons to keep Jordan. They had kids and we kept them sometimes, and we were actually owed a couple of overnight sleeps, which was the big thing with Jordan and their boys lately. Sometimes Jordan had to call us at bedtime and be reassured, but all in all he didn't mind. And by the next day, we would practically have to pry the kids apart to get Jordan to go home.

Ann took Jordan to their house while I sat watching TV, but really listening for the phone. Wanting it to ring. Wanting to get on with things.

Nothing happened.

Ann came back and we finally went to bed about ten and made love, which wasn't too good because she was still mad at me. Or mad at Jim Bob really, but I was handy. She said something about, "I'll make that goddamn bastard think *snag my panty hose,*" a couple of times before we gave it up for the night and she rolled into my arms and I held my hand between her legs and buried my nose in the fragrance of her hair. And just as I was drifting into sleep, the phone rang.

I got to it without turning over the nightstand and groped it off the hook and coughed something into it.

"Get on up here," Jim Bob said.

"Yeah," I said. "Coming."

"You awake?"

"About half-ass."

"Well be whole-ass by the time you get here, got me?"

I said something and lay back down. Ann rolled over and put her arm around my chest. "Jim Bob?"

"Yeah. We've got to go meet him."

"Does that mean we don't have time for a quickie?"

"He didn't say anything about a time limit," I said.

Our lovemaking was rushed, but Ann wasn't mad anymore, and it was better than when we had spent more time. I knew why.

We were both scared.

22.

Jim Bob and Russel met us out in the parking lot.

"We'll take the Red Bitch," Jim Bob said.

Ann and I got in the back and Russel got in front with Jim Bob. It occurred to me that if Russel and Jim Bob were pulling our legs, they might be taking us out to the river bottoms to dispose of us. It could be that way. Russel and Jim Bob had been friends for a long time, and I hadn't any idea what Russel had really said to him on the phone. I wished I had thought of that before now. I looked at Ann, and as the lights from stores and buildings slanted across her face and made her fine profile show there in the car, I got the feeling the same thoughts had occurred to her. I figured that if that was the case, her last words to me would be, "I told you so."

We drove on out of town and as we did I looked over the Red Bitch real good. The upholstery was red and on the dash in up-raised blue-silver letters was JIM BOB. The steering wheel was covered with a tacky, false cheetah skin and an emerald-colored suicide knob the size of a doorknob was fastened to that. Jim Bob liked to drive with his left hand on the knob and his right hand across the back rest. I could see a little of his face in the rearview mirror. He looked happy as a drunk.

"How are we going to dig him up?" I asked. It had occurred to me that I hadn't seen any shovels, and that was making me even more nervous.

"Got some shovels and stuff in the trunk there. All manner of tools. Damn near everything's back there in the trunk but another car."

"Maybe we could use another," Russel said. "This ain't exactly one to be sneaking around in."

"Who's sneaking, goddamnit. We're driving. Ain't no crime in driving. Hell, I have a pickup, but I didn't bring it."

"No joke," Russel said.

Jim Bob looked over at Russel and grinned. "Want to see me lose this cop?"

Russel grinned back. "I thought you were losing your touch. I noticed him when we left the Holiday Inn. They switched cars on us."

Neither Ann nor I had looked back to see the car that was supposed to be following us, but it was tempting.

"Are you sure it's a cop behind us?" I said.

"Oh yeah," Jim Bob said.

"Can't he just pull us over?"

"What for, driving a red Caddy? That ain't no crime."

"Perhaps this one ought to be," Ann said.

Jim Bob laughed. "Lady, I like you, I really do."

"If we run, won't the cops be laying for us?" I said.

"Well, we ain't gonna just run, we're gonna lose him legal like. But before I do, could you folks tell me where the hell this grave-yard is?"

"The other direction," Russel said.

"Figures," Jim Bob said, and he took a left in the Safeway parking lot just in front of a big tractor trailer rig. The car that was tailing us went by. Or I assume it was the one. When I got the chance to look, I saw a sporty blue Plymouth slow down and fall over to the left-turn lane. But the traffic was thick and he couldn't make the left.

Jim Bob got back on the highway by rushing out front of a yellow Volkswagen that honked its horn and flashed its lights. It whipped around on the left and came even with Jim Bob. A husky college boy on the right-hand side rolled down his window and flipped Jim Bob the bird and yelled something.

Jim Bob waved at him friendly like, put his foot to the floor and the Red Bitch jumped forward. Jim Bob whipped in front of the Volkswagen again, went around another car and made the right lane. We went fast like that for two blocks, then Jim Bob took a right, then a left, then a right and a left again.

"Am I going in the general direction?" Jim Bob asked.

"General," Russel said.

"Good enough."

"We lose the cop?" I asked.

"Oh yeah," Jim Bob said. "Them and their little toy cars. Whatever happened to the good ole days when it was the biggest, meanest car on the road, not the smallest and the cheapest?"

"The Arabs is what happened," Russel said.

We finally got out to the graveyard, and Jim Bob killed the Red Bitch and went around and opened the trunk. I stood there wondering if we were about to be killed, but the trunk was just like he said. Full of tools. He got out two shovels and a long canvas bag and put them on the ground. He gave Ann the keys.

"You take the Red Bitch on down the road a piece and kill the lights but leave the motor running. Turn it facing this way, though, so you can see what's going on in case something goes on. We're gonna try and make this quicker than a bunny fucks—pardon me again."

"Would you quit saying that?" Ann said.

"You know, I'd rather," Jim Bob said. "What say if we're gonna be waltzing partners I just let fly when I need to and consider me sorry for what I say. If I don't cuss I get all filled up inside just like I was constipated and I don't feel worth a damn."

"I sure wouldn't want you all constipated with cuss words," Ann said. "But listen, I'm not a taxi."

"No, ma'am, you ain't, but we're gonna do the digging and someone's got to do the driving, and I'm running this shindig, so do what I say."

"But we're paying," Ann said.

"And it's money well spent," Jim Bob said. "You can't do no better than me. Now let's get on with this."

Ann looked at me and I shrugged.

"Okay," she said.

"Take it easy on the clutch," Jim Bob said as Ann got in.

"I can drive," Ann said. She closed the door and started the car and drove down the road a ways, backed around, pointed the lights at us and killed them. The Caddy was just off the road and under an oak. When the lights were out, you couldn't see it. It was that kind of night.

"They can wrap you up for quite a few years for grave stealing, can't they?" Russel said.

"Hell, they can throw away the key," Jim Bob said.

We went over to the graveyard fence and found the gate un-locked. "Reckon they don't expect folks to come in much," Jim Bob said, "and the ones here ain't going nowhere."

Russel located the grave and I took a shovel and Russel took one.

"What about you?" Russel asked Jim Bob.

Jim Bob opened the canvas bag and took out a long flashlight. "Hell, someone's got to hold the light."

Russel and I started digging. While we were at it, it began to turn off cool and it got darker. You could smell rain in the air. When we were about halfway down to the coffin, it began to sprinkle.

"Better get with it," Jim Bob said. "I think it's gonna come a real frog strangler, and if it does, you're gonna have to bail as well as dig."

"How's your back?" Russel asked Jim Bob.

"Fine," Jim Bob said. "How's yours?"

"Hurts. I'm using a shovel," Russel said.

"And you use it so well."

Russel began digging faster, and as we got close to the box, his digging became more frenzied. I looked over at him once, and what light was on him made him look like a corpse. He was afraid of what we would find down there. His son and his hopes in a box.

I looked over at Jim Bob, and since he was holding the light, I couldn't make out his features too well, but he seemed more solemn than I'd yet seen him. He was also quiet for a change.

Russet's shovel scraped the coffin.

We began cleaning the dirt off and around it. Throwing it up high and over. It was getting to be harder work. The rain was coming down faster and the clods were sticking together and becoming heavy.

"All right," Jim Bob said, and he jumped down on the coffin with his light and canvas bag. He stepped off the box and found a place to stand between the coffin and the grave wall, and he opened the bag.

"There's more to tapping these babies than just opening a lid," Jim Bob said. "They seal these fuckers but good nowadays. You got to have the right tools. Fortunately, I got them."

He pulled some strange instruments out of the bag and turned to look at Russel. "Whatever's in here, I don't want nothing crazy out of you. If it's your boy, I'm sorry, but you move to cause Dane here trouble, and I'll wrap this damn tool around your head."

Russel smiled grimly. "You'll try...but don't worry. I haven't nothing against Dane anymore."

"Well, just in case you get something suddenly," Jim Bob said, "remember what I told you."

Jim Bob applied the tools to the coffin and in a moment the lid popped up with a whoosh of air, like one of those cans of vacuum-packed peanuts, and there was the body. It was in a hell of a shape. It looked like someone had taken a can opener to it and stitched it up with black cord while drunk. The eye I had shot out was stuffed with what looked like wax, and it hadn't been done neatly; the body looked like something out of a monster movie.

"Ain't much to look at," Jim Bob said, and he put a hand on Russel's shoulder.

Russel looked quickly at the face and said, "Hold the light on his right hand."

Jim Bob did that and Russel picked up the corpse's right hand and looked at it. "You remember my boy, don't you Jim Bob?"

"When he was little," Jim Bob said. "He was blond, wasn't he?"

"Hair can be dyed...but this isn't him. Freddy had a cluster of little, pale moles on the back of his right hand that looked like a four-leaf clover...like these." He let go of the corpse's hand and held his own in the light. I could see the faint pattern of moles on the back of his powerful hand. I was surprised I hadn't noticed them before.

"You're sure?" Jim Bob asked.

"More than sure," Russel said.

I was feeling sick. "From the looks of him," I said, "you'd think they purposely tried to mess him up."

"I think that was the idea exactly, sport," Jim Bob said.

That hadn't occurred to me seriously, and now that Jim Bob said it, I felt that this whole thing was even deeper than I expected. A conspiracy. Little obstacles all along the way. Maybe they expected the body might get dug up at some point, and wanted to make it hard to identify. And maybe an autopsy on a body that no one is expected to see isn't performed for points on neatness.

I tossed my shovel out of the hole and climbed out after it. I had had enough. Jim Bob shut the coffin, stood up on it and took my hand and I pulled him up.

Russel followed. His big hand took mine and I yanked him up, and as I did his eyes looked straight at me. I couldn't tell what was in them, but it wasn't threatening.

I took my shovel and started throwing the dirt in furiously. Russel grabbed up the other shovel and joined me. Jim Bob held the light.

We threw the dirt in at random, then we found our stride and began shoveling in unison, shovelful per shovelful. We got faster and faster. I could hear Russel grunting beside me and the smell of his sweat and the light rain was on the wind and I began to feel loose, even strangely comfortable. There was nothing I wanted to do more in the world at that moment than cover that hole.

Finally Russel and I had it finished and we patted our shovels on the earth as if by signal.

We looked at each other.

"Anybody ever quits wanting to dig graves around here," Russel said, "I think we could get a job."

I grinned. "Probably."

Lights pinned us against the night and doors slammed and I looked toward the road. I could make out that it was two pickups, and I could see four men getting out of them with baseball bats. They went around in front of the trucks, which they had parked across the road facing us, and stood framed in the lights.

One of them nervously, or perhaps eagerly, tapped his bat against the side of his shoe. He called out, "What'er you fucks doing out here?"

"Paying our respects to Uncle Harvey," Jim Bob said.

"This time of night?" the voice asked.

"It's the time of night we get the most sentimental," Jim Bob said. "What about you boys, you out here for a little batting practice?"

"You might say that," the voice said.

"That's kind of what I figured," Jim Bob said. "Don't reckon you boys would listen to reason?"

"Sort of doubt it," the voice said.

"Yeah, well, remember, I gave you your chance."

One of the men laughed, then they all came toward us and started through the gate.

"What do we do?" I asked.

"Simple," Russel whispered to me, "first asshole within range, you see if you can crease his head with that shovel."

"It could kill him," I said.

"Let's hope so," Russel said. "Those bats won't do us much good, I can promise you that."

"Is there any good reason for this?" Jim Bob asked. "I mean, what have we done to you boys?"

"Not a thing," the speaker said, and then he rushed Jim Bob with the bat.

Jim Bob was standing slightly in front of us, and he dropped the flashlight and turned in the direction of the grave, I thought to take the blow on his back, but he kept going down and he spun and his leg shot out and caught the first man on the ankle and knocked his feet out from under him and the man hit the ground and the bat went up and fell down heavy end first and struck him between the eyes and the man yelled.

Jim Bob was on his feet then, and the second man was nearly on him and the bat was coming down. Jim Bob went straight to the man and ducked under the bat and the bat waved uselessly over Jim Bob's shoulder and Jim Bob grabbed the man's throat with one hand and uppercut him in the balls with the other, then he twisted his hip into him, slipped an arm around his waist, bent, and sent the man flying. Jim Bob didn't even lose his hat.

Russel stepped forward and faked a shovel blow to the third man's head and the man brought the bat up to block and Russel dropped the shovel low and hit him in the kneecap. The man barked and went down.

The last man made a run for the trucks. He was nearly in the middle of the road when the Red Bitch came barreling down on him and the lights came on, then the Bitch braked, but the car still hit him and sent him over the hood. He rolled up against the windshield and flipped over on the driver's side. He tried to stand, I guess, because the door came open, and at the same instant the inside light framed Ann, the door made impact with the man hard enough to make my testicles pull up.

The men from the pickups were down and I hadn't done anything but hold a shovel.

The man Jim Bob had thrown was trying to get up, so I looped my shovel over casually, not putting much force behind it, and let it come down on his head. It made a nice, comforting ring on contact.

"See you're still messing with that Jap stuff," Russel said to Jim Bob.

"Korean. Hapkido. Hey, Dane, that wife of yours. She ain't got a sister at home, does she?"

23.

I went around and threatened the others with my shovel and told them to lie down with their hands out in front of them, which they did. The one Russel hit in the kneecap was yelling his leg was broke, and the one Jim Bob swept the feet out from under was complaining of his ankle. You would have figured they thought we were the Red Cross.

The one I hit with the shovel wasn't saying anything. He was out cold. And so was the one Ann popped with the Caddy door. She was standing outside the car now, leaning on the open door, looking over the roof at us. She waved at me and I waved back. It was all very pleasant.

"Sorry we had to whip the shit out of you," Jim Bob said to the moaners on the ground, "but we didn't have much choice. We're gonna leave now, but first, just to clear up a little mystery, just what are you fellas doing here?"

Neither answered.

Jim Bob went over and kicked the man with the kneecap injury in the hurt leg and the man howled like a wolf. "Now let me rephrase that in exactly the same goddamn way. What you doing here?"

"A man hired us to come out here and see if anyone was messing in the graveyard," Kneecap Injury said. "He said if there was someone, we should beat them up good. He paid us."

"What did he look like?" I asked.

"Tall, good-looking guy. Like a cigarette or clothes commercial or something," Knee Injury said. "Had on a suit. Not the kind you get at J. C. Penney's."

"Where'd this fella find you boys?" Jim Bob asked.

"Tonk outside of town called the Wagon Wheel," Knee Injury said. "Come on man, give me some peace. I'm hurting."

Jim Bob walked around him and kicked him in the other leg, then walked over and kicked the other guy in his good ankle. "That'll help balance the pain. Next time you come to fuck with me, sweeties, you better bring your daddies. You goddamn boys ain't worth a fuck."

They lay on the ground and moaned.

"Tell you now," Jim Bob said, "we're gonna be going, and I'd like y'all to lay right where you are, else I'm gonna feed those ball bats to you. Got me?"

A couple of nods.

"Y'all have a nice night," Jim Bob said, "and since this rain is sort of clearing up, if you'll watch right over there, when that cloud cover clears, you ought to be able to see the Big Dipper."

When we got over to the car, I went around and looked at the man Ann whopped with the door. He was groaning and starting to get his hands under him so he could get up. I took hold of the door and jerked it forward again and popped him in the head. This just wasn't his night. He went out like a light. I was beginning to feel a little savage, though I didn't have any right. So far, all I had done was pop two guys in the head who were already down and threaten a couple who were injured. I was some tough guy.

"Is everything okay?" Ann asked. "They aren't going to die or anything are they?"

"You done good," Jim Bob said to Ann, "and they're all okay. Fellas over there think their legs are broke, and they might be right, but it's better than what I'd like to do to them."

Ann looked down at the man she hit with the car. "Did you see him fly through the air?"

"With the greatest of ease," Russel said.

Jim Bob took the keys from Ann and went around and opened the trunk and put the shovels and the tools in it. He slid back a part of the trunk bottom, reached inside and took out a double-barreled, sawed-off shotgun.

"You're not gonna finish them, are you?" I asked.

He laughed at me, walked over to one of the pickups and shot the front tires out. He broke open the stock of the shotgun, rolled out two more shells, reloaded, went over to the other truck and did the same.

Turning toward the graveyard, he yelled out to the guys, "They were damn near bald anyway."

He put the shotgun back in the trunk and we got in the Red Bitch and Jim Bob put the pedal to the metal and we were gone.

When we got back to the Holiday Inn we went up to Jim Bob's room. He took off his shirt, which had been torn somehow in the fight, and started to put on another. Ann said, "Is that a chicken tattooed on your chest?"

"Chicken?" Jim Bob said. "It's an eagle."

"It looks like a chicken," Ann said.

We all leaned forward. It did look like a chicken.

Russel said, "I've always thought it looked like a chicken."

"I was drunk when it was done, but I didn't ask for no chicken. It's just faded some is all."

"It wasn't faded when I first saw it," Russel said, "and I thought it looked like a chicken then."

"To hell with the chicken," I said. "Price set us up tonight. The description that guy gave was Price. He went in and hired those men to beat us. I just don't know how he knew we were at the cemetery."

"He didn't," Jim Bob said, snapping the snaps on his shirt. "But he thought it was a good possibility. He's trying to discourage us. It's just the sort of thing that makes me mad. But we know one thing. The body in that hole ain't Freddy. Next step is to find out where Freddy is and who the hell is in the hole. And why all this shindigging."

"And how are we going to do that?" I asked.

"For the time being, leave that up to me."

"So what do we do?" Ann asked.

"You and Dane go home and do what you always do. Normal business. Go to work. Go home. Go to work. Regular shit. And Dane, I'd like you to hire Russel to work at your place. Ben said you owned a, what is it?"

"Frame shop," I said.

"Yeah, you put him to work so he isn't a vagrant, and I'll put him up here at the Inn. Just pay him a token salary and count it out of what you owe me. Keep it cheap, though."

"I'm not sure I like this," I said.

"I'm not wild for it either," Russel said.

"We gonna get this done," Jim Bob said, "we're gonna do it my way, or you two can do it yourselves or just forget it. I'm curious and I want to do this for Ben, but I'm gonna call the shots or it ain't gonna happen. It's not like I'm making any big fortune off this."

"I'm paying you," I said.

"It ain't my regular fee. Lot of this is coming out of my pocket, and I can tell you now, if you want to stay in business, you don't work that way. You don't buy the frames for your clients, do you, Dane?"

"I'm not asking you to work cheap," I said. "You settled on a fee—"

"I'm not complaining. I'm just saying money isn't what's keeping me in this. But I'm not going to stay at it unless I'm calling the shots. That's how it is."

"All right," I said, "I'll take him on, but let's don't drag this out."

"It takes as long as it takes," Jim Bob said. "Ben can start working for you in the morning. In the meantime, I'll get on the next step here. You want to check in and see how things are going, great, give me a call. But this is gonna take some time and I want to be left alone as much as possible."

"That's it then?" Ann said.

"For now, Lady," Jim Bob said. "So let's say good night, or damn near good day, and go home and sleep. You skipping work today, Dane?"

"Yeah."

"Good. You look like hell. Tomorrow Ben starts working for you."

"Nine o'clock," I said.

Ann and I stood up.

Jim Bob shook our hands. "Just go on about things regular like."

Russel offered his hand to me, and after a moment, I shook it. Then he offered it to Ann.

She looked at it for a long, hard moment.

"I don't think so," she said.

He nodded and put his hand by his side. "I don't blame you," he said.

"It wouldn't matter if you did," Ann said.

We went out. On the way home it started to rain again. This time very hard. It continued that way throughout the day and most of the night and the morning after.

24.

A day's rest hadn't helped me much. I was still tired on the morning I started back to work. Depressed too. The idea of having Russel around me all day was not appealing.

To make the situation even more confusing, he reminded me more and more of my father. It wasn't just the massive hands. He moved like my father and I fancied their voices were much the same.

And perhaps there weren't that many similarities, and I was merely trying to raise the ghost of my dad and give him substance.

But if that was the case, why couldn't I have chosen a more suitable host than a goddamn ex-con who threatened my child and nearly beat my brains out?

The morning was already hot, as usual. The rain had quit only a few hours before and the sun was out now and boiling the wetness off the brick streets like the damp off a beached fish's scales.

I had to pass in front of the shop before I could make the turn that led to the lot in the rear where I parked and as I passed, I saw Russel standing out front, leaning on the glass door. I had hoped to at least have a little time to get unlocked and get the coffee brewing before I had to deal with him.

I went on around back and parked and opened the shop and went through to the front door and tapped on it. Russel jumped a little, and I unlocked the door and let him in.

"Snuck up on me," he said.

"I drove by out front and saw you. I thought maybe you saw my car."

"No, I was woolgathering. Nice place. It looks like you get some business."

"Yeah. We do all right."

I led him to the back and told him to take a chair and I put on coffee. When I was finished with that, I turned the thermostat to a cooler level and went over to the cash register and unlocked it. I had the bag of money I'd brought from home, just enough small change and dollars to get us rolling for the day, and I put all that in the register.

"What is it you want me to do?" Russel said.

He had left his chair and was standing at the counter.

"I don't really know," I said. "I haven't thought about it. I guess you can clean up."

"All right. With what, and how do you want things done?"

I took him to the back and showed him the closet with the broom, mop and dustpan. I showed him the bathroom. "You can get water from here for mopping," I said. "Somewhere in that closet is a bucket and there's some soap and all manner of stuff. I'm not even sure what's in there. We're not too good at cleaning up, actually."

"I noticed," Russel said. "There's glass and wood and sawdust all over the floor under the work tables."

"Yeah, well, we're busy. You just do what you like, but look busy. I don't want to make James and Valerie feel like I'm playing favorites."

James and Valerie came in then, and they looked at Russel, then looked at me.

"New employee," I said. "I've hired him for a little while to kind

126

of straighten the place up, since we don't seem to get around to it." I hesitated, wondering if I should say Russel's name. It didn't seem likely they would remember who it was I was supposed to have shot, and even if they did, it was even more unlikely that they would associate the last names as kin. "This is Ben Russel."

James shook Russel's hand and Valerie smiled, which was good as a hug any day. She seemed to like what she saw in Russel, and it was obvious Russel didn't mind looking at her either.

"Well," I said, "let's get to work."

Russel straightened the closet first, then swept and mopped the joint until it was as shiny as the White House silverware. When he wasn't working, he talked to Valerie, and they got along just fine. A lot better than James got along with her. It burned James so bad he came up front and leaned on the counter and whispered, "What's that old guy got that I haven't got?"

"A hard-on?"

"Funny, boss. You're a riot. Maybe you should get your own television show."

After about a week, I got fairly comfortable with Russel. I even praised his work. I wanted to hate him, but I kept finding myself liking him. Now, when I looked at him, I didn't get the vision of him on my son's bed clutching the boy's pajama top in one hand and holding a knife in the other. I couldn't associate the man that night with the man working for me. I saw a man that reminded me of my father. And that made me uneasy. I'd force myself to remember what he'd done so I could get mad. But the anger wouldn't last.

I got so content with him, I'd slip and say things about him at home. Nice things. Maybe something funny he'd said or done, and when I did, Ann would look at me as if I were a priest who had just announced the best use for a crucifix was scratching your ass. But I couldn't help admiring the old guy. He was a character. He had style. Like the way he handled Jack the mailman.

Since our little run in, Jack had been less than friendly. He would deliver the mail by opening the door, giving us all a look that could turn bricks to shit, then toss the mail across the floor hard enough to send it sliding halfway across the shop.

I kept thinking he'd get over it, but finally decided I was going to have to confront him, or call his supervisor. But Russel took it out of my hands.

One Tuesday after Jack had done his trick, Russel came over and said, "So what's with him?"

I didn't want to bring up the night of the shooting, but I didn't see any way out of it. I told Russel everything. It actually felt good to talk about it and get it off my chest. As the days had gone by, the incident, like a lingering chest cold, had built up inside of me again. I was sleeping lousy, snapping at Ann and Jordan, and thinking about the bad things in my life more than the good; it was a relief to let the poison out.

"I see," Russel said when I finished, and he went back to work.

Wednesday at mail time, Russel was up front, waiting by the door, smoking a cigarette. It didn't occur to me what he was planning until an instant before it happened. Jack came walking along like clockwork, opened the door, stuck a mail-filled hand in and cocked his wrist in preparation of a toss. But Russel grabbed the hand and bent it back and stepped outside with Jack.

Russel put his arm around Jack's shoulders, and Jack shrugged sharply, but the arm didn't go away and suddenly Jack and Russel were moving past the display window and out of sight.

I got nervous and went outside, and at the corner of the building I found Jack's cap and our mail, and when I went around the corner I found the mail pouch and Jack and Russel. Jack was on the ground and there was a trickle of blood running out of his nose.

"This is against the law," Jack said, "fucking with the U.S. Mail."

"Next time," Russel said, "I'll shit in your cap and make you eat out of it. I expect you to deliver the mail right from here on out. Got me?"

Russel's voice had been so low and straightforward, it scared me. It was the tone he had used that day in the parking lot of the day school.

"Yeah," Jack said. All the bravado had gone out of him. He was just a big bully that had finally met his match.

"You aren't so tough," Russel said. "I'm a sixty-year-old man and I just kicked your ass. Get up and git."

Jack rolled to his hands and got up. He saw me standing at the edge of the building and he turned red. I handed him his mailbag as he walked by.

"Don't forget to pick up that mail you dropped," Russel said. "Deliver it the way it's supposed to be delivered. Now."

Jack turned around and looked at Russel, and there was a hint of showdown in his eyes. But just a hint. It faded like an ice-fleck on a stove.

"Now," Russel said in that menacing voice.

Jack swallowed, went around the corner, got his hat and picked up our mail. We followed him and watched him open the door and drop the mail inside, gently.

"Very nice," Russel said.

Jack squared his shoulders as best he could, and walked past us. Before he was out of earshot, Russel called after him. "You have a nice day, hear?"

25.

Lunch time I drove Russel over to Kelly's, ordered hamburgers, fries and beers. I couldn't help myself. There was something about the guy.

After lunch we had a couple more beers and Russel said, "I'm going to ask this straight out. You feel any different about me, Dane? I guess I'm saying, do you forgive me?"

"Does it matter to you?"

"It matters."

I thought a moment. "I don't know exactly how I feel. Obviously part of me likes you, or I wouldn't be here with you buying you lunch and shooting the breeze with you."

"Part of you."

"I feel guilty liking you. Maybe I like you because you remind me of my father, or the way I remember my father. He killed himself when I was very young. Then, there are times when I think about that night you had hold of Jordan with one hand and had a knife in the other. You didn't use it, but I still think about it. It's like a snapshot in my head."

"You know what I saw when I was holding your son's shirt that night, Dane?"

"No."

"My son. For some reason I saw Freddy, or the way I remember Freddy. I haven't seen him since he was a boy, except that picture of him older that his mother sent me in prison. I don't know if I really remember that much about him, or if I made it up in prison. But that's what I thought of that night. Freddy."

"Tell me about Freddy," I said.

"I don't know if there's any more to tell. His memory is more like a parasite than anything else. It eats at me. He had little hands, blond hair, the same freckles on the back of his hand that I have."

"And blue eyes."

"Yeah, and blue eyes. I remember noticing that he had such little hands. Not just little for a baby, little hands. Not deformed, just small. My mother had hands like that. She also had the freckles on the back of one, just like me and Freddy. You know, the last thing I really remember about him is sort of sappy. It was Christmas and I bought him a red truck and I remember him on the floor playing with it. Even now, when I think of him, that's the first thing that comes to mind. I have to look at the older picture of him and concentrate real hard to imagine him any older than five, and then I don't do it so well."

"What was the fly in the ointment, Russel? What happened?"

"I was the fly. I think from the day I was born I've been damaged goods. No bad cracks, but some hairline fissures. My dad was a night watchman at a factory and my mother took in sewing, later she had her own shop. They made a decent living and they were decent people. I can't blame them for a thing. They did everything they could to encourage me, put me off in the right direction."

"But it didn't work?"

"Nope. I just couldn't stick with anything. I got bored. I wanted everything now, not later. I didn't like starting at the bottom. I always felt smarter than everyone around me, and I didn't like some redneck asshole standing over me telling me what to do when they didn't know what to do."

"We all think we're smarter than the other guy," I said.

"I thought it more than others. I know better in a way, but hell, I still think that deep down. There's a part of me that just can't understand why I've got to go the slow route like the Philistines."

He drank some of his beer and smiled at me. "I'm a case, aren't I?"

"Yeah, but you don't sound so different from a lot of others. That still doesn't explain what happened."

"Maybe it's just a lazy streak Dane, I don't know. But I'd be working in some factory, making some machine mash aluminum pipe into lawn furniture, and I just couldn't see beyond that. It was like whatever it was I was looking for was hiding and it could hide real good. I felt like I had been sent to hell. You know what hell would be to me, Dane? Working in an aluminum chair factory, mashing that goddamn monotonous aluminum pipe into chairs, the sound of those fucking machines going, cachump, cachump, and some redneck standing over me telling me to do it faster. That's hell to me."

"Lot of people have done shit jobs," I said. "Me included. You don't have to do them all your life."

"I don't doubt that, but for me I could never see beyond them. No future window, I guess. As time went on I started feeling empty, and then I got into the quick money."

"Stealing?"

"Yep. I didn't get caught when I was young. Just luck, no other reason. I fell in with some guys and we knocked off filling stations all over East Texas. Carried water pistols that looked like guns and we'd split the take. Even then I felt it was just something I was doing until I found what it was I was supposed to do. The thing that would take that part of me that was empty and fill it up."

Russel raised his beer very deliberately and took a long, slow sip from it.

"To shorten this story up," Russel said, "I didn't stop doing it, and I did a little stretch later on for a grocery store robbery. I went in with my water pistol and the owner had a pistol under the counter, and his didn't shoot water. He just held the gun on me while one of the clerks called the police. I did some time. Not much. I was young and the judge was lenient, and they didn't know how long I'd been robbing places. To them it was my first offense.

"Anyway, I graduated to the big time when I got out. I went to Florida and got in with this professional hotel robber named Mick. He had a perfect scam. He had bellboys and elevator operators on his payroll, and when a good mark checked in, they'd call him."

"Just business to them."

"Exactly. Then he and I would come over at the right time, go to the mark's room, beat the lock, which is something I got good at—"

"I know."

"That guy gypped you. Those locks and bars he gave you might keep a twelve-year-old kid out, but any burglar could go through that stuff like a worm through shit. You ought to get your money back."

"I'll keep that in mind. What about the Florida stuff?"

"We'd go into a room and take what we wanted, put it in the mark's suitcase to add insult to injury, and just walk out. We knew all the back routes and we had the inside help. It was nothing. Got so we were making big bucks."

"But you weren't satisfied?"

"Nope. Same old story. I couldn't see beyond what I was doing. I always wanted to, but couldn't. It was like the moment was it, and once I realized that, everything just sort of closed in on me. Robbing beat the hell out of factories, but after a while it just didn't do it. And I could never get over the guilt. I wasn't really a born criminal. I couldn't rationalize it the way Mick and others could.

I always saw it as wrong. My upbringing, I guess. I mean I knew I was a crook and a sleaze. I didn't feel like a debonair cat burglar, I felt like a scumbag. One time we were robbing this hotel room, and on the way out I saw myself carrying the suitcase full of loot in one of those full-length mirrors, and it hit me. It was like a picture of my life and I didn't care for it."

"So you tried to reform."

"Yes, I did. I came back to East Texas. I met Jane and we got married. I started working at a plywood plant, and for a while there, the work didn't bother me. I had someone to come home to and something to expect. Then when Freddy was born, things began to fall apart. I wanted things for the little guy and I couldn't see it happening at the plywood plant. I got a little promotion, but it was so piddling it just made me mad. Like I said, I've got no patience. I want everything now. Thinking back on it, I was doing pretty good there and the promotion came pretty quick, and the next one would have too. I'd have been off the line completely and I'd have been the redneck telling the other poor bastards what to do. But I got empty again and started fucking up. I stayed mad all the time and it showed at home and work, and I got demoted and I quarreled with Jane and yelled at Freddy enough that I felt guilty. And that's when I started doing the little jobs. I'd take weekends and go case places outside of town and I'd steal little piddling things. I mean, it wasn't helping my income much, but it gave me some kind of purpose. Damned if I can explain it. It's like that guy that keeps rolling the rock up the hill in hell. Gets it to the top and almost over, then the bastard rolls back on him. My life was like that. I'd almost have it whipped, then it would roll back on me."

"Did your wife know?"

"She suspected something. Me going off on the weekends, saying I was hunting or fishing. I never came back with nothing. I didn't even go to the fucking fish market and buy fish to bring home and fake it. It was like I wanted to be stupid. If I had gone to the fish market, I'd probably have bought fish sticks just so I could look even more stupid.

"Finally I robbed the payroll at the plant. It came in late one evening and I knew all about where it was kept by then, so I came back that night, beat the lock and the safe and stole it. One of the bosses just happened to come back for something and he saw me going out of the building. Next day it didn't take them long to put two and two together. They let me off with giving the money back and firing me. They didn't want any stink."

"Sounds to me as if you were lucky."

"That's a way of looking at it. Anyway, you know the rest. I finally got in with some guys and did a job on a liquor store and that one cost me about twenty years. Jane tried to stay in touch, and for a while I answered her letters, but I wouldn't let her come visit. I didn't want her and Freddy to see me in prison. I still didn't feel like a convict. I felt persecuted. Can you beat that? I kept thinking they'd come to their senses and let me out."

"She sent me pictures of Freddy and kept me informed about what he was doing. Said he did well in school and played football and was a quarterback. Seemed to be good at everything. I was proud in one way, but in another I felt like the shit at the bottom of a dog pile. I even burned her letters and some of Freddy's pictures. Decided to just let them go so they could build a life that was worth something. It was like I had gotten worse than empty. It was like the bottom had come out of me and there wasn't anything on the other side of me, just a hole to nowhere."

"What about your wife?"

"She hung in there for a long time. She loved me. I quit answering her letters and for a time she still wrote, but finally she quit. With the last she sent that picture of Freddy as a young man. I never heard from her again. I learned later that she died drunk in a motel in Dallas. I don't know anything else about it."

"Freddy?"

"No idea. But I made up my mind when I got out I was going

to find him and make it up to him. I was going to mend the hole in me and fill it up with something. Then when I got out I was told he was killed, burglarizing your house no less, and there wasn't just a hole in me, Dane, there was a vacuum that sucked out my soul."

"And now that you know I didn't kill him?"

"Maybe the hole's closing up. I've got some hope. I don't know who that sucker is in the ground out at the graveyard, but it isn't Freddy. That means there's a good chance he's out there somewhere, and I want to find him and be some kind of father to him. Convince him that loving me is worth something. And convince myself that my life hasn't been just a waltz of shadows, that it has purpose. Or can have."

"I hope it works out, Russel. I really do."

"I know you do."

I ordered coffee, and we drank that and had another cup. I said, "You talked to Jim Bob?"

"Tried to, a couple of times. He's not saying much. He told me to put my faith in the Lord and Radio Shack."

"Radio Shack?"

"That's what he said. He's not going to say anything until he's ready. I've known him a long time. He's a lot smarter than you think he is. Don't let that hick front and all those corny good-old-boy sayings fool you. Back when I was doing the robberies, he knew. He tried to straighten me out, give me some good advice. But—"

"You didn't listen."

"I knew he was making sense, and I still couldn't listen. Same old story. Know better, but can't do better."

I looked at the clock on the wall.

"Damn," I said. "We need to get back to work. I doubt James and Valerie would like the idea of me taking the hired help out to lunch and beers and chitchat while they're building frames."

I put down the tip and paid the check and we got out of there.

Back at work I sat behind the counter and thought about Russel back there sweeping up; thought about what he told me about having a hole in him that made a vacuum that sucked out his soul.

26.

It was a hot Sunday with a hot wind blowing through the pines like a diseased cough, carrying a hint of dead fish from Lake LaBorde. The birds were making small talk in the trees like it was more of an obligation than a desire; they sounded like they needed air-conditioning.

I know Ann and I did. We were taking turns leaning over the backyard grill cooking hamburgers and wishing we'd fixed tuna-fish sandwiches inside. Jordan was taking it well enough though. He was sitting on the patio playing with a toy car and making motor sounds.

I'd just flipped the meat when I heard the phone in the kitchen, and I went inside to answer it.

It was Jim Bob.

"What'er y'all doing?"

"Grilling some burgers, sweating like peasants."

"Sounds good."

"The sweating or the grilling?"

"Both, I reckon. I been in this damn room so much I need a

JOE R. LANSDALE

good honest sweat. The bottoms of my feet are starting to grow carpet."

"Well, come out."

"Can you put up with Russel too?"

"Jordan's here, and...well, you know what happened."

"I know, but I've got something important to tell the two of you. Can you make some kind of arrangements? A baby-sitter?"

"It'll be a little inconvenient, but I guess I can talk to the Fergusons. They still owe us a few baby-sittings."

"Good."

"This news you want to tell us. Is it good?"

"Good? Well, I don't know if it is or not, but it's news. I've made some headway. I know what happened to Freddy, and I know how to find him."

"That's good news."

"Not necessarily."

"Is he alive?"

"I think so."

"Isn't that good news for Russel?"

"Maybe, maybe not."

"What's all the mystery, Jim Bob?"

"It'll be easier to explain when I get there. I'll bring some beer."

"Good enough. See you in a while."

"By the way, I like mine well-done. When that sucker is smoking it's cooking, when it's black it's done."

"One hockey puck coming up."

The burgers were done long before Russel and Jim Bob arrived, and we set them in the microwave until we wanted to warm them up again. We fixed Jordan his, and he ate, and I called the Fergusons and asked if it was okay if we brought him over. They agreed and Ann drove him there and came back madder than when she left—and that was pretty mad. She didn't want Russel over for dinner. In her mind, it was like inviting Hitler. What she wanted was to jab him in the eye with a pointed stick and nail his head to a post.

Maybe put turpentine on his balls and light it. Just to be contrary, she said we'd eat outside on the redwood table. She wouldn't have that man in her house—again.

By the time they showed the wind had turned savage and stale and the mosquitoes, like bomber squadrons, had started to move out of the woods in search of prey. But it was getting late enough that the sun was moving westward and the grill had cooled, so it wasn't as hot as it had been. Instead of quick frying, we were simmering.

I heard the Red Bitch come into the drive, and I went around and met them and led them around back. When Russel saw Ann he began having trouble with his hands. He didn't know where to put them. He tried by his sides and in his pockets, but they didn't seem to fit or hang right, mostly just fluttered about as if trying to escape from his wrists. I'd never seen him so flustered as when he was in Ann's presence.

Jim Bob didn't seem to notice. He held up a six-pack of Lone Star and Ann took it and put it in the fridge inside. She started the burgers microwaving. I had Jim Bob and Russel sit down at the redwood table, and I went inside and got the fixings and brought them out on a tray.

Ann brought the burgers and some beers, and we each fixed our buns with mustard, lettuce, tomatoes, the whole shooting match. The only one that really did any talking was Jim Bob. He talked about the weather and the price of gasoline and about how the LaBorde police had been following him around like a baby duck following its mama, then he turned to Russel and said in the same tone of voice, "I found out what happened with Freddy, Ben."

Russel paused, tried to find what he wanted to say. "Is he—"

"Far as I know he's right as rain in the health department, but I'm not sure you're gonna like what I have to say."

"Say it," Russel said.

"All right. There's a whole flock of ways to find a missing person, and if I don't know all of them, I ain't short of the rest of them by more than one or two, and I figure if they were any good I'd know them."

"You don't lack for confidence, do you?" Ann said.

"No," Jim Bob said. "I know what I can do, and what I can't do, and one of the things I can do is find people. It ain't because I'm such a smart sumbitch, though I guess I'll do in a pinch, it's because I got connections. You get lots of connections when you been in this business long as I have. But I'll get to the connections later.

"I moseyed down to the newspaper here for starters. Figured as this was Freddy's last known stomping grounds, least according to the police, might be mention of him in the papers somewhere. Not just counting obituaries, damn near everybody shows up in the rags eventually, in some manner or another, so it's a good place to start. Same method of research you used, Ben, when you were finding out about Dane here."

"Don't remind me," Russel said.

"Yes," Ann said, "don't remind us."

"I went over to the paper to see what I could turn up, and damn if I didn't find a couple mentions of Freddy. One of them was about Dane shooting him, which we know he didn't, since it was some other poor bastard, and that one didn't get front page, but it didn't get last page neither. It was placed a little too casually in the middle. Meaning, they wanted a lot of people to see that dude, but not get the impression they were advertising. It wasn't a big article and it didn't go into details, but it managed to mention Freddy's name four times."

"Just in case someone might miss it," Ann said.

"Yep," Jim Bob said. "The paper, or whoever was instructing the paper, wanted to be right sure someone out there thought Freddy had bit the big one. That's why the cops took advantage of this burglar thing and tagged the body with Freddy's name. If Freddy's dead, then there's nothing but a cold trail, and ain't no use in anyone looking for him."

"Why would anyone be looking for him in the first place?" Russel said.

"Getting to that. I said I found two mentions of Freddy. Other was about a month earlier. Said one Freddy Russel was going to turn state's evidence on a bunch the paper called the Dixie Mafia."

"Hell," I said, "I remember seeing that. Went in one eye and out the other. And I sure don't remember Freddy's name."

"No reason you should. That article was tucked on a back page and was about a paragraph and Freddy's name was mentioned once. I'm sure if the FBI had its way, it wouldn't have been mentioned at all. But they took some pains to correct that a month later when they gave that dead burglar Freddy's handle."

"The FBI?" Russel said.

"Those are the fuckers behind all this," Jim Bob said. "That's why Price let you out, Ben. It was the wiser thing to do under the circumstances. They didn't want you and Dane raising a stink that would point to Freddy again. Price is probably like most local law. He don't give a damn for feds, but he's got to grease their assholes if he wants to or not. And when this burglar came up colder than a carp, he saw what the FBI was looking for. A goat. And better yet, the fucker's killed right here in Freddy's own town. It's a match made in fucking heaven's what it is. His identity for ole Freddy's. The guy you killed, Dane, probably didn't have a family or anyone he could be hitched to easy, so they gave him Freddy's name."

"Okay," I said. "But I still don't understand why."

"What I got from that little paragraph in the paper," Jim Bob said, "is that Freddy was with these Mafia types, doing whatever Mafia types do, and things got shitty and the shit got over his head, and the law came down on him, and to keep from getting mashed under their boot heels or those of his ole buddies, he sang like a fucking parakeet with a hot coat hanger up its ass."

"And in return," Russel said, "they gave him immunity."

"Uh huh," Jim Bob said, "and they went him one better. They didn't announce it, but it seems logical to ole Jim Bob here that since the dead Freddy ain't the right Freddy, they had plans for the right Freddy all along. They tucked him underground. That was probably part of the deal all the time. Freddy agreed to sing for a new identity, and the FBI went for it, and when he was through with the concert, they pretended to let him free for a time, when he was in fact hidden. So the Dixie Mafia is running around looking for him so they can skin the hide off his balls, and not too long after, this asshole breaks into your house, you shoot him—"

"And when I ask Price if he knows him, he says yes on the spot and sticks him with Freddy's name," I said.

"Bet he did know him," Jim Bob said. "Knew enough about him to think he could get away with it. Saw what the feds were needing, and maybe Price saw a promotion out of it, a feather in his cap somehow. He called the FBI, told them what had happened and what he had done, and the big boys went for it. If they'd hated his idea, he'd have called you back and said it was all a mistake. The fella killed wasn't Freddy Russel after all. He just thought it was 'cause they looked a little alike, and—"

"None of this would have happened," I said.

"That's the size of it," Jim Bob said. "Price has been trying to cover his and the feds' tracks ever since."

"I'm beginning to understand how my wife died like she did," Russel said. "She was lying to me about Freddy. He was trouble all along."

"Like his old man," Ann said, and if you could sharpen words and throw them, hers would have gouged out the back of Russel's head about a foot.

Russel looked at her and there was no sarcasm in his voice when he said, "Just like him."

"You know where Freddy is, don't you Jim Bob?" I said.

"Yep," Jim Bob said. "A lot of what I'm telling you was guess-work at first. Just me looking at a thing and putting it in line with my experience and coming out with what seemed likely. But

I've verified it all, and found out some more since, and I do know where he is."

Russel got out a cigarette and lit it. I noticed his hands were trembling slightly. Your own flesh and blood can do that to you.

"If you know," Russel said too casually, "then the Dixie Mafia can find out too, can't they?"

"Maybe," Jim Bob said, "But they got to have the right connections. And I think if it was that easy for the witnesses to be found, there wouldn't be any relocation program. The FBI folks may not be Einsteins, but they ain't as dumb as the news people want you to think. And they're pretty damn loyal—least to one another. They might tell someone they trust something they shouldn't, but most of them wouldn't give a thug the time of day. And if things start looking bad for their witnesses, the people they've relocated, they usually move them. That's not to say they hang out with the people they move night and day. They don't. They get them set, let them go, and give them a number to call if they have problems. They're pretty much on their own after that. But that's because the FBI has pretty good faith in its relocation programs. Once in a while there's a hole somewhere and a bug gets in the batter, but not much. They hide a lot of folks when you get right down to it, and most of those folks stay hidden."

"What kind of connections do you have?" I asked.

"Ben," Jim Bob said, "you remember Calvin Hedges?"

"Arrested me for drinking a couple of times over in Smith County. Kept me overnight and let me loose. Hell, I was just a kid then. He still alive? He must be eighty years old."

"Eighty-five," Jim Bob said. "Claims his pecker still gets hard as a screwdriver. He isn't sheriff anymore, but his boy Calvin, Junior, works for the FBI, and old Calvin owed me a couple of big favors. I called in one of them.

"I had him phone his boy and have the boy call me. Took a couple of days to arrange it on account of Junior was out of pocket, but he did call and said he'd do me the favor."

"Pretty agreeable, wasn't he?" I said.

"Like I said, his old man owed me a couple of favors, and the boy wanted to help pay them off. One of the favors the old man owed me had to do with Junior his ownself, and Junior knew it. He also knows I'm one of the good guys, and he was willing, after a line of bullshit, and me putting it on him pretty hard about how he and his old man owed it to me, to tell me what I wanted."

"Freddy's location," I said.

"Wasn't that easy. He wasn't gonna put his neck in the noose that far. But he works in the records department and he gave me an access code to the central FBI computer. That's kind of like a gal giving you the key to her apartment. I got another code or two from him and.... Well, to make this a little easier on you folks, a computer, if you know what you're doing, is a sneaky booger. There've been fifteen-year-old kids that knew how to use them and managed to break codes as tough as the Department of Defense. It takes time to do something like that, but you can damn sure do it. You got to first get some of them low-level access computers to give you what you need, and you use them to move up to the superusers. And if you're real good like me, and you can get the codes you need without having to hunt for them, you can save yourself a lot of time and wiggle in there like a snake, and get what you want with less chance of getting caught with your drawers down. Them computers are something. You take one of them dudes and a modem and you can damn near do anything but walk the dog with 'em."

"You know how to do all that?" Russel said. "You know about computers? Where'd you learn that?"

Jim Bob looked hurt. "A manual, you jackass. Hell, I'm smart as a whip. You know that. And I got sense enough to know you got to keep up with the times. Just because man was born with his butt hanging out didn't mean he had to stay that way. He made clothes out of a bear's hide, then cotton, then that synthetic shit. Same way with computers. That's how things are now. You don't keep up, it's like some gal using the rhythm method instead of the pill. It don't make sense."

"Or," Ann said, "it's kind of like a man depending on a woman for birth control instead of caring enough to do something about it himself."

"All right," Jim Bob said. "You got your lick in. That too. And besides, you can get these little games to go with computers, and they're neater'n hell. They got this one with this monkey that climbs a ladder and throws coconuts, and there's all sorts of traps and pitfalls for the monkey, and it's a challenge, that's what I'm trying to tell you. There's some others I been wanting to try, but they don't just give those dudes away, you know."

"Guess this is what you meant when you told Russel Radio Shack, huh?" I said.

"Yeah. And by the way, you just bought yourself a computer and modem for your business, I don't need one. I got a big system at home."

"I don't want to buy a computer, and you said your fee didn't count expenses."

"I consider this an exception," Jim Bob said.

I started to argue with him but decided it wasn't worth it. Jim Bob was like a force of nature. If you were going to deal with him, you had to accept the consequences. The hard part would be dealing with Ann later. I hoped I could convince her my business needed a computer. I refused to look at her; things would be bad enough with her after they left.

"All right," I said. "I roll over. Tell us what you found out for Christsakes, and just get on with it."

"Bottom line," Jim Bob said, "is he's in Houston, using the name Fred Miller. The question now is, do we want to take this thing any further." Jim Bob turned to Russel. "He's your son, Ben, and it's your choice. If you want to find him, we'll do it. If not, we'll just let it go, find out what Dane wants to know and the rest of it is so much wind."

"He doesn't sound like what I had in mind," Russel said.

"He's your son and you've come this far," Jim Bob said, "and now that he's away from that Dixie Mafia bunch, maybe things could be different. I don't think he's gonna be singing no hymns or nothing, but he might turn out all right. He might not even have been into anything real bad, just found out some real bad things. Maybe he squealed 'cause it was getting on his conscience.... On the other hand, things could turn out a lot worse than you can imagine."

Russel looked at me. "If you still have a mind to finance me so you can find out what you want to know too, then I'm for going on."

"Can't turn back now," I said. "I've got to know."

"See it through no matter what it costs you, huh?" Ann said.

I looked at her. "Sorry, but yeah."

She shook her head but didn't say anything.

"All right then," Jim Bob said, "we do it. Tomorrow night, late, we leave this chickenshit town. I got me a promise to keep tomorrow, and I won't be free till late."

"What kind of promise?" Russel asked.

Jim Bob grinned. "Well, I promised this sweet little thing that works at the hotel restaurant that she could have my undivided attention all day, and I don't break my promises. Besides, it wouldn't be gentlemanly to deny her what may be the most rewarding experience of a lifetime."

"I said it earlier," Ann said, "and I'll say it again. You don't lack for confidence."

"Ain't that the truth," Jim Bob said.

27.

I woke up about three in the morning and rolled out of bed and sat on the edge and thought about the dream I'd had. I couldn't quite recall it, no matter how hard I tried, but it had been dark and dreary and very sad. There were tears on my face. I think maybe I dreamed I died and no one cared. It didn't make much sense.

I sat there thinking about it, and Ann rolled over and touched my back.

"You've got to see this thing through?"

"I do," I said.

"I just have this horrid feeling it's all going to turn out so ugly, baby."

I didn't tell her I felt exactly the same way. It was like I was a toy windup soldier pointed in a direction I couldn't alter. I had no choice but to go until I wound down. The thought of being driven made me think of Russel, his dissatisfaction with life, the feeling that there was a hole in him and his soul was rushing out of it and he didn't know if he could get it back. How did that happen? Could it happen to me?

"You'll be careful?" Ann asked.

I turned back onto the bed and took her in my arms and pulled her to me and smelled the scent of her so strongly that there were tears in my eyes.

A man without a soul didn't have anything to cry about, so I considered the tears a good sign.

"Please tell me you'll be careful," Ann begged.

"I will," I said. "I'll be careful."

"Jordan and I love you. We need you."

I had needed my father, but he had left me. My mother had left me and I had needed her. I couldn't remember either of them ever needing me. I thought of Dad holding me that last time and looking at me and telling me he loved me.

"Jesus," I said.

"Make love to me," Ann said. "Don't worry about anything. Just make love to me."

I kissed her and did just that. When we were finished, I lay there holding her. She smelled wonderful, an aroma concocted of perfume and sweat and sex. There in the bad light she looked very young, like the girl I had fallen in love with so many years ago. Her skin seemed smooth and untroubled by lines of worry, just the way it had been when she was young and things were simple and sleep canceled out all pain.

I nuzzled in her hair and felt her warmth and solidness, felt myself filling up again with life and soul and everything that was good.

But I knew it wouldn't last.

Damn me, I knew it wouldn't last.

PART THREE
FATHER AND SON

28.

When I awoke, I was disoriented. The world had been spun around and my bed had shrunk during the night. I started to call for Ann when I realized where I was. On the outskirts of Pasadena, Texas, at Jim Bob's house in the spare bedroom. Jim Bob was upstairs and Russel was asleep on the couch in the living room.

I sat on the side of the bed and scratched my head and thought about coffee. Last night seemed like a dream, a bad dream. We had left LaBorde about midnight, and I had fallen asleep in the backseat of the Red Bitch, awakening as if from a violent mugging.

I remembered sitting up in the seat of the car as we went over the Ship Channel bridge and seeing the water and ships out there and later the foundries as we entered Pasadena. There was something grim and alien about those places with their smokestacks chugging dark, stinking loads to the sky, and every time I saw those foundries, especially at night when great spurts of fire shot skyward from tall, narrow pipes to mix with the foul smoke, I was reminded of Dante's Hell. I thought it must be dreadful to work at those foundries, out there in all that heat and smoke and stink, those chemicals and boilers constantly cocked for disaster.

The thought of all that put me back down in the seat, and I drifted off to the sound of Jim Bob and Russel talking about old times, their words losing meaning, becoming a drone, having an effect on me not too unlike a mother's cradle song. When next I understood a word, it was Jim Bob tugging my shoe and calling my name, trying to get me awake.

After that I remembered carrying in my little bag and Jim Bob's house being large and lonely and smelling of dust. The room he put me in was not so large, and it had a little bed and a tiny air-conditioner that strained frantically to put some cool into air that had been dead for days.

Now it was morning and I was awake and it was damn near cold and I had a stomach that wanted breakfast, a body that wanted coffee, and a brain that was trying to put together exactly how I had gotten myself into all of this and why.

I looked at my watch. Ann and Jordan were not up yet. Another hour and they would be going through the morning routine and Jordan would be spilling his first glass of milk for the day. Damned if that didn't suddenly seem endearing.

Most likely Ann would wake up mad at me and stay mad all day. She had agreed to let me go and had given me therapeutic sex the night before, but in time she would get mad again. She'd think about Russel and how foolish I was, and she'd be hot as those pipes at the foundry that shot out the fire.

James and Valerie would run the shop well enough, but James would moon over Valerie's ass something disgraceful. He might do it so much he wouldn't count change right.

Maybe Jack the mailman, with Russel gone, would start throwing the mail again.

I got up and stretched and felt the worse for it. I put on my clothes and went out into the hall and through the living room where Russel was lying awake, looking at the ceiling, smoking a cigarette.

"You too?" he said.

"Just got up," I said.

"I couldn't sleep," he said.

"I slept, but it wasn't worth a damn. I guess I dozed too much in the car. I don't do so good after midnight anymore."

"Older you get, the worse it gets," Russel said.

"If it can get any worse than this," I said, "you might as well kill me now."

Russel threw the covers back and stood up. He had on pale gray shorts with a triangular design down the inseam; his belly hung over the waistband as if slowly melting. His arms, back and shoulders were covered with gray hair and his face looked long and creased with lines. His chest seemed to have fallen in like the roof of an old house and his posture was bad. Only his arms and hands looked strong. It was as if old age, mad as hell, had crept upon him during the night and climbed inside his skin.

"Let's find some coffee," Russel said, lighting a cigarette.

He slipped on his clothes and coughed some smoke and we staggered along to where the living room quit and became the kitchen. Russel found a Mr. Coffee, and after rummaging through the cabinet, a can of Folger's and some filters.

"Maybe there's something to eat in the fridge," he said.

I went over and looked in the refrigerator and found some thick bacon wrapped in wax paper and some eggs. I put the stuff on the counter and got some bread out of the bread box and put it in the toaster and chased down a frying pan. I opened up the bacon wrapper and put all the meat in the frying pan and started stirring it with a spatula.

"Best way to cook that is naked," Jim Bob said. I turned and there he was wearing his jeans and no shirt, that stupid-looking chicken on his chest, his big feet bare and awkward looking without his boots.

"Naked, huh?" I said.

"Yep," Jim Bob said. "Get a little hot grease popped on your balls and you learn to turn that fire down." He came over and turned my fire down and took the spatula and went to moving the bacon around. "How'd y'all sleep?"

"Not too good," I said, "but it wasn't the accommodations. I just had a lot on my mind."

"Same here," Russel said.

"That's too bad. I slept like a hog on ice."

We ate breakfast and the bacon was great. Best I'd had in years. I asked Jim Bob about it.

"Came from my hogs," he said. "I raise the squeally fuckers. I'll take you out and show them to you after awhile. Got a wetback takes care of them for me. I get these eggs from a fella down the road. Got his own chickens and he doesn't let them peck shit, but then he don't put them in no boxes and force-feed them neither."

"What about Freddy?" Russel asked abruptly.

"We go check on him," Jim Bob said.

"We've got to find him first," I said.

"No problem. New phone book just came out, and since he's new in town he's bound to have a phone. I mean, he ain't Freddy Russel no more. He's got a new life and new name and the FBI has given him a new past."

Jim Bob got up and went over to the phone book and opened it. "There's a lot of Fred Millers in here, but that ain't no sweat neither. We'll check the old phone book and look and see which Fred Miller has been added to this new listing."

Jim Bob put the open phone book on the table and went away and came back with another phone book and opened it. He put it on the table beside the new one and compared. "Here we go," he said. "Only one new Fred Miller in the book, and now we've got his address."

"You're sure it's him?" Russel said.

"Sure enough," Jim Bob said. "We'll check it out."

"Too easy," I said. "I'd never have thought of that."

"That's why I'm the fucking detective and you build frames,"

Jim Bob said with a sly smile. Then he turned to Russel. "You going to try calling him, Ben?"

"He's probably at work," Russel said.

"You've got to do it sometime," Jim Bob said. "We've gone this far, you might as well go the whole hog."

"I think I'd like to sort of look in on him without him knowing. I just can't pick up the phone after twenty years of not even trying to answer letters his mama wrote or writing him or anything."

"Just doing it would get it over with," Jim Bob said. "In the long run, I think that would be the easy way."

"I guess it would for you," Russel said. "But he's my boy and I haven't treated him like he was anything to me. He may not even know I'm alive or care. I just couldn't do it straight out."

"All right," Jim Bob said. "We'll spy on him some until you get your nerves up."

"You make it sound like some kind of showdown," Russel said.

"Well," Jim Bob said, "in a way, ain't it?"

Russel nodded. "What say you take us out there to look at those scrawny hogs of yours, Jim Bob?"

"If you guys promise not to diddle them," Jim Bob said, "they're kind of shy."

So we went out and looked at these hogs of Jim Bob's, and he must have had twenty, plus some piglets. They were huge things, white and big-eared and Jim Bob said they were called Yorkshires.

The hogs were housed in a roomy, air-conditioned building that had a flap door so they could go out into a big, fenced enclosure if they wished. There was the ripe smell of dung and urine in the air, but it wasn't bad. The hogs were raised clean, and Jim Bob said the wetback, Raoul, came around once a day and changed the bedding and checked the water connections and made sure there was feed in the automatic feeders. When the hogs got fat enough, Jim Bob sold them, saving one for his own freezer, and some for breeding stock; now and then he replaced his boars and litter sows with younger more sexually ambitious swine he bought and brought in, so his bloodline wouldn't foul, as he put it.

Out behind the hog house, he showed us a big wood and chicken-wire cage full of soiled hog bedding. "That's my compost pile," Jim Bob said. "Me and Raoul pull this crap out of the hog house and stack it here and let it heat up, and come spring it's broken down and ready to spread. I hire this colored fella I know, Henry, to bring his mules over and bust up my land. Then me and Raoul, when he hasn't been sent back to Mexico for a while by the Immigration, spread it around and plant early as we can. Pig shit, if composted right, can grow anything. Raoul keeps saying he's gonna try putting a pussy hair out there and growing him a woman, but the only pussy hair he can get hold of is his wife's and he damn sure don't want another one of her."

We walked down behind the compost pile and out into Jim Bob's garden. We went between rows of corn with stalks nine feet high and bright green. There were mounds giving birth to squash plants with white pattie squash on them big as the crown in a cowboy hat. There were thick tomato vines staked on sixfoot poles, and the strong, fine smell of the tomatoes was enough to make your nose hairs twitch. The tomatoes were firm as hardballs and red as a wound. Jim Bob picked us each one and we walked along the rows eating the warm, juicy tomatoes and marveling at the cucumber vines that ran renegade throughout the garden with cucumbers on them that Jim Bob said were "as big as Big Tex Dildoes."

When we got to the far end of the garden, we turned left and walked around the edge of it, then started back between a row of turnip greens. The greens were thick and green and looked more like Venus flytraps than turnip greens. By the time we were out of the garden and heading back toward the house, I felt as if we had been expelled from the Garden of Eden.

29.

"That's Freddy's house right there," Jim Bob said.

It was late afternoon and the bottom of the sky had turned the color of a burst tomato and the gray was pushing it down and away. But we could still see where Jim Bob was pointing. We were across the street and about a half a block down from Freddy's house. It was just a house. Light pink brick on a street full of houses built just like it, but some with gray and some with red brick. The lawn was mowed and I could see the knob of a sprinkler out in the yard. Freddy watered his grass. I wondered if he had a barbecue grill out back, and maybe a dog called Boscoe that had his own house with his name painted over the door.

"It could be another Fred Miller," Russel said. "We don't know this is Freddy." There was something almost hopeful in Russel's tone. I didn't know if it was the years that were bothering him or what his son had become, or what he himself had become. Maybe all those things.

He shook out another cigarette and lipped it, lit it with his Bic lighter and inhaled, and about a quarter of the cigarette glowed and went to ash.

"You're supposed to smoke those, not suck them," Jim Bob said.

"What you need's a straw and something to drink. And this is Freddy's house. I'll bet my left nut on that."

"I don't want your left nut," Russel said.

"How about my right? I keep it a little cleaner."

"Ha, ha," Russel said, and sucked up another chunk of the cigarette and the ash fell off in his lap.

"Hey, watch the upholstery, and open a goddamn window," Jim Bob said. "I feel like I'm in the fucking gas chamber."

Russel brushed himself and the seat and rolled down his window and blew a mouthful of smoke out of it. Just watching him do that made me feel hotter than I was. The air-conditioned air in the car had died immediately when Jim Bob shut off the engine, and the air outside was only slightly less stale. At least it wasn't full of smoke. I rolled down my window and stuck my head out and took a deep breath. It warmed my throat and lungs and made me thirsty. When I was finished with that, I pulled my sweaty shirt away from my back and leaned forward and said, "Now what?"

"Yeah, Ben," Jim Bob said. "Now what?"

"I don't know," Russel said.

"You're costing Dane money here," Jim Bob said. "He's footing the bill."

"Nah," I said, "that's not the problem. I just want to do something. I'm getting itchy."

"I just can't do it yet," Russel said.

Jim Bob sighed and rolled down his window. "Maybe you'd like to drive down to the other end, turn around, see the house from that angle."

Jim Bob meant the comment sarcastically, but Russel, who wasn't fully tuned in, said, "Okay."

Jim Bob looked back at me and rolled his eyes. "All righty," he said, and he rolled up his window and Russel and I did the same. Then he cranked the car and the air-conditioning panted through it and we went coasting down the street.

When we reached the dead end, Jim Bob backed the Bitch

around as slowly and carefully as if it were made of eggs, and started back up the street.

Russel hadn't even looked at the house when we passed it, and he didn't act as if he were going to look this time. He had his eyes glued straight ahead.

"If we can get the colors of the house coordinated with the sprinkler knob," Jim Bob said, "maybe we can buy Freddy some nice lawn furniture or something. A pink flamingo maybe."

Jim Bob was going so slow and was so busy giving Russel a hard time, he didn't notice the garage door at Freddy's house going up or the blue Chevy Nova backing out of it down the short drive at top speed. I barely saw it, and by the time I yelled, the car was on us. The back of it hit the Red Bitch on the right-hand rear door, and sent my nonseatbelted self flying across the car.

I put my hands on the seat in front of me and straightened to a sitting position. Jim Bob had killed the engine and was cussing "Goddamn idiot, I'll kick, his motherfucking ass."

"It might be Freddy," Russel said.

"I don't give a damn if it's God," Jim Bob said, opened his door and got out.

Russel turned around and looked at me. "You okay, Dane?"

I rubbed my neck. "I think so. But maybe I should yell whiplash."

I looked at the car that had backed into us and saw the driver's door open and the driver get out. And get out. And get out. He was as big as King Kong, Mexican, and had a look on his face like he'd eat shit and sugar before taking a beating from anyone. Jim Bob included.

Jim Bob was almost to the Mexican, but his steps were a little slower. He stopped about four feet away and cocked his hat back.

Russel rolled down his window, said softly to me, "I've been waiting to see this. I even thought about this in prison. I've wanted to see Jim Bob get his ass kicked all my life. He never has that I know of."

"Hey, Frito," Jim Bob said, "ain't they got no fucking mirrors in cars where you come from, huh? What the dog-shit is wrong with you, man?"

The Mexican just looked at him. He was wearing a tight-fitting, blue Hawaiian shirt with yellow and red palm trees on it He had on yellow slacks and big, black wing tips with olive explosions on the toes. He was nearly seven feet tall and his chest was like a beer barrel.

"You talk to me?" he asked.

"No, fucking Chili Lips, I'm talking to the goddamn Nova. It looks the smarter of you two. Did you see what you done to my car there? Fucked the paint job. Look at that."

Jim Bob turned to point and the big Mexican (a.k.a. Frito and Chili Lips) stepped forward and grabbed the brim of Jim Bob's hat and pulled it down so hard Jim Bob went to his knees. Then the Mexican kneed Jim Bob in the face sharply.

"We ought to help him," I said.

"Shit," Russel said. "Look at the size of that guy."

The Mexican had Jim Bob by the back of the neck now and the seat of the pants and was using him to punch the door on the Nova.

"Too far," I said, and got out of the car. On the street side, I stood and yelled over the top of it. "Hey. Quit that."

The Mexican looked at me like I was crazy, then went back to jamming Jim Bob's head into the Nova.

I went around the car, not real fast. "Now that's enough of that," I said. "Quit."

The Mexican dropped Jim Bob on the drive and said, "Okay. You do." Then he said something in Spanish. It was brief and as menacing as his English.

I didn't run. I stood there.

Had to. My feet were glued to the ground. Seeing him come toward me was akin to watching some natural phenomenon, like an eclipse. He was almost on me. I put up my fists. Not that I thought I'd get to use them much. I just hoped it was short and painless.

Russel opened the door of the Bitch and got out. I didn't see him, but I heard him. At the same time Jim Bob got up. He had a look on his face that was more embarrassed than peeved.

"Say, you want to try that again, Taco Ass," Jim Bob said, "only with me looking this time?"

The Mexican turned to look at Jim Bob and Jim Bob said something in Spanish and waved Russel away with a hand. "Just me and him."

I backed away and to the side. I could see the Mexican's face that way. He was smiling. It was a nice smile, like the kind sharks must get before they go for the dangling leg of a swimmer.

Then Jim Bob moved. He sort of skipped sideways and his right leg folded up and his foot shot out, and the heel of his boot took the Mexican in the balls, the leg half-folded and the foot shot down and hit the Mexican in the knee.

The Mexican screamed. Jim Bob's foot whipped up again, and his leg went high and arched back and his heel hit the man behind the temple with a crack like a wooden ruler being snapped.

The man fell down and didn't get up.

"Shit," I said. "He isn't dead is he?"

"Hell no," Jim Bob said. "I ain't wanting to hurt the shithead any worse than a beating. He ought to watch where he's backing."

Jim Bob found his hat and put it on and winced. "Owww. Man, he was trying to put me through that door.... Thanks for wanting to help, Dane. And fuck you, Ben."

"I sure hated to see you whip that bastard," Russel said.

Russel went over and rolled the Mexican on his stomach and got a wallet out of his back pocket and opened it and looked for identification. He read what he found and put the wallet back. He said, "There's a little sap in his back pocket too. Be glad he didn't take that out."

"I am," Jim Bob said. "That identification didn't say he was called Fred Miller, did it?"

"No, smart ass, it didn't," Russel said.

Jim Bob walked up to the house and rang the doorbell. Russel shook out a cigarette and stood with it unlit between his lips, watching the door. No one opened it. Jim Bob knocked. Still no one opened it.

Jim Bob came back and went over to look at where the back of the Nova was pressed against the Bitch. "You look at that? My fucking rear door is totaled."

"Get the license plate number if you want to fuck with insurance," Russel said.

"After I kicked his ass?" Jim Bob said. "No thanks. I might have to kick it again, and I'm not sure I can. Shit, look at that."

He walked over to the Mexican and grabbed the man's pants leg and pulled it up a little bit, revealing a small holster with a small revolver.

"I'm glad he wasn't in no O.K. Corral mood," Jim Bob said.

"Let's go," Russel said, "neighbors might have seen us."

Jim Bob went back and looked at his car. "Damn." Then he glanced at the Nova. The trunk hood was bent up and knocked open. Jim Bob looked inside. "A movie lover," he said.

I went over and looked. There was a small box of videotapes. They had little stickers on their spines and the names of movies written on them. Some of the movies were Mexican, some were English and American. One of them read *Star Wars*. Jim Bob reached that one out of the box, held it up.

"I'll just call the beating I gave that sumbitch and this here my insurance settlement. Ain't enough, but it'll do."

We got in the car and Jim Bob drove us out of there.

30.

We had some hamburgers and fries at a McDonald's and sat in a back booth and considered things. There was a lot to consider.

"Well, as the little ole lady asked," Jim Bob said, "what the fuck does it all mean? Who was that big Meskin and what was he doing backing out of Freddy's garage late afternoon with a trunkload of videotapes, and is he evidence that you can still buy driver's licenses at Sears?"

"Maybe your detecting is off, and that isn't Fred Miller's house," Russel said.

"That's his house, and you know it," Jim Bob said. "I don't fuck up that bad."

"It doesn't seem that mysterious to me," I said. "Freddy has a friend who's Mexican, and the guy has run of the house and he was over there for whatever reason and he just happened to have his movie collection in the trunk of his car. Maybe he shares the place with Freddy. Could be a way to meet the bills or something."

"When you get right down to it," Jim Bob said, "it don't matter. What matters is that our friend, Ben, here, ought to just call Freddy up and get it over with."

"I don't feel comfortable doing that," Russel said.

"You're not going to feel any more comfortable about it tomorrow," Jim Bob said.

"Maybe not," Russel said, "but I'll know when I'm ready."

"He'll know," Jim Bob said. "You get that, Dane? He'll know. Shit."

We went on back to Jim Bob's place, and Russel didn't talk much. For that matter, neither did Jim Bob, and I wasn't chatty myself. Jim Bob tuned in a country and Western station and sang along with the songs a little, and damned if he wasn't pretty good.

At Jim Bob's house, Russel went to take a bath and Jim Bob got us both a beer and I sat on the couch and Jim Bob took a chair next to the television.

"I don't know about you, pardner," Jim Bob said, "but I'm so bored I could sing to my dick."

I was trying to visualize that, and having some trouble, when Jim Bob said, "Hey, let's watch that damn movie. *Star Wars.*"

"It's good," I said. "But it looks better on the big screen."

"Get me a big screen and we'll play it on that," Jim Bob said. "But in the meantime, I'm gonna play it on that nineteen-inch RCA there. You don't mind me watching it do you?"

"No. I wouldn't mind seeing it again."

"Good, 'cause I was gonna watch it anyway."

Jim Bob had left the video out in the Bitch and he went through the garage and got it. When, he came back he had a dark scowl on his face. "Man, that Nova screwed the Bitch good. I'm gonna call a man I know about getting it fixed tomorrow."

Jim Bob went over and slipped the cassette into the VCR and turned it and the television on. "I got some popcorn," he said. "I could fix us some."

"I could always eat popcorn," I said.

The video crackled and popped and there were ripples. Jim Bob started to get up to make the popcorn, but he hesitated. "Looks like a bad copy."

"You'll want to turn it off to make the corn anyway," I said. "This stuff with the big spaceship at the first is pretty fine."

But there were no credits and no Star Wars. There was bad video camera work with a young Mexican girl sitting on a bed with her hands and feet tied.

"What the hell's this? This ain't *Star Wars* is it?"

"No," I said. "It looks like some sort of cheap porno tape."

Then the big Mexican Jim Bob had fought stepped into the camera's eye. He was naked and sexually ready and looked even bigger without his clothes.

"Shit," Jim Bob said, "home movies of the Mex and his old lady."

The Mexican went over to the girl and pushed her back on the bed and undid the binding at her feet and spread her legs and got on top of her. The girl didn't fight. She was very complacent. Only her eyes suggested she didn't like what was happening.

The Mexican didn't waste any time, and when he finished he stood up by the bed and another man stepped into view. He was naked too. He was a head shorter than the Mexican and not nearly so wide and sporting a little paunch, but he still looked powerful. The camera angle switched then and we got a closer look at his face. He had thinning, blond hair and blue eyes and nice teeth and he was showing all of them. The camera went back to its original side-view angle and the blond man got on the girl and did what the Mexican had done. When he was finished he grabbed the girl by the hair and pulled her to a sitting position on the edge of the bed and she let out a little squeak like a mouse with a brick on its tail. The blond man put out his hand and a hand off camera put a little revolver in it. The girl understood suddenly what was going to happen and she tried to lift her bound hands to her face but the man with the gun was too quick and he shot her in the forehead. Blood leaped out the back of her head and went all over the bed and she fell back in it with her arms out, kicked briefly with one leg like she was jump starting a motorcycle and wet herself. The urine pooled under her and blended with the blood and her left eye rolled up in her head and her right stayed fixed as if it had discovered something unique on the ceiling. The camera went close on her face and the hole in her head was tiny as the width of a dime with a bead of blood pushing out of it. The blond man's face came into view and he licked the bead away and rolled it around in his mouth as if tasting wine.

Static replaced the picture. Jim Bob reached out and cut the video off. He turned to me and his voice was hoarse. "That was for real. An honest to God snuff film."

"He's older, heavier, and losing some hair," I said, "but he still looks like his photograph, and when he took the gun—"

"The moles on the back of his hand were shaped like a four-leaf clover."

31.

"Don't say anything to Ben," Jim Bob said. "Not yet."

He got the cassette out of the machine and turned off the television. He went over to the bar in the kitchen and got a pen and paper and wrote a note.

"I'm telling Ben we've gone to town for some beer," Jim Bob said. "You and me got to talk."

He put the note on the table and took the cassette with him out to the garage. We got in his black Dodge pickup instead of the Bitch. We backed out and drove along through the night with the cassette lying between us like a bomb. We didn't talk for a time.

"Maybe it wasn't real," I said. "It could have just looked real. They can do anything now."

"It's okay to be hopeful, Dane," Jim Bob said, "but there's no use in being stupid. It was real."

We drove on in silence until I said what we were both wondering. "What about Russel?"

"Poor bastard can't get a break, can he?" Jim Bob said. "It isn't like he hasn't gone through hell. And now this. Ain't nothing could be worse than having your kid get killed, unless it was finding out he wasn't a human being."

"What's it all about, though? Why would he do that?"

"You're having a stupid attack again. Freddy enjoys it. Did you see his face? You don't lick blood out of a gunshot wound unless you enjoy it. And I bet he's gone into the movie business kind of regular. Stars himself and the Mex and some little gal that won't be missed much. My guess is he brought her from across the border somehow. Smuggled her over. Some whore he paid, told her he was going to take her to a big party, and all she had to do to make an extra couple thousand was fuck a few of his friends. Only it was rougher than that. Christ, how old was that gal, Dane?"

"I don't know. Fifteen?"

"Yeah. That's about what I figure. I bet that ain't the first gal he's aced or the last. Tapes like that he can sell to the sicko trade for big bucks and be reasonably safe about it. Them ain't the kind of films the owners invite the neighbors over to see. That crap is for sick shits to sit in the dark and jack off to."

"Jesus, people would pay to see that shit?"

"Live in the real world, buddy. There's people who'll pay to see anything. Buy tapes of girls shitting in each other's faces, dogs fucking them in the ass, or just what you saw. We ain't talking stuff for an Elks smoker here. I heard of a rich man once on the other side of Houston that bought tapes of operations, animal experiments and war atrocities, and he could do that legal. I wouldn't doubt he's got some stuff like we saw on this here," he touched the tape with a finger as if poking a monster to see if it were dead, "in a vault somewhere. Maybe that's how he gets it up so he can fuck the old lady. He can pretend he's gonna shoot her after he gets off—"

"I get the picture," I said.

Jim Bob pulled off to the side of the road suddenly, as if his hands wouldn't hold the wheel anymore. He held them out to me and said, "Shit. You look at that? I'm shaking like a virgin bride."

We sat there for a time with the motor running and the lights on, and Jim Bob said, "We could ditch this tape, tell Russel I fucked up on the Fred Miller stuff, that my FBI contact was full of bull doodoo, and that it wasn't a cover for Freddy after all. I could pretend to look some more, and after a while, give up. Say I couldn't find any leads. He needn't never know."

"I wouldn't believe that story if you told it to me," I said. "Not after knowing you just as long as I've known you. You wouldn't give up. You're too egotistical."

"True."

"But even if we could get away with doing that, that wouldn't change what we saw or what Freddy's doing, would it?"

"No. He'd keep right on keeping on."

"Does that matter to you?"

"Damn sure does. I think the scumbag ought to be tied to the highway and have a semi-truck driven over his head."

"So what do we do?"

"Damned if I know," Jim Bob said.

We drove on to town and got the beer and when we got back Russel had the couch folded out and was sitting up in bed smoking a cigarette and watching the tail end of the news.

"Got some beer," Jim Bob said, holding it up.

"That's nice," Russel said. He looked at me. "And you went with him."

"Yeah, I went with him."

"For beer?"

"Yeah," Jim Bob said, "beer."

"What are you two homos really up to?"

"Beer," I said. "Can't a man go out and get a goddamn beer without being hassled?"

I walked past the couch and went to my room and closed the door and sat on the edge of the bed. I thought about the tape and the young girl and the Mexican and Freddy. I thought about the gun and the blood and the urine. I closed my eyes and tried not to think about anything. I wasn't good at that.

I thought about Ann and Jordan, but that made me more ill than comforted.

I got up and went out again and passed by Russel's couch.

"You got jock itch, Dane?" Russel said. "Settle down, you're making me nervous."

"I want to walk, all right," I said. "Okay if I do that? Am I gonna get penalized or something?"

"Don't get on the rag," Russel said. "It's just you're making me nervous. You and Jim Bob are acting like kids that got caught jacking off or something."

"I'm just homesick," I said. "Jim Bob, can I use your phone upstairs to call? I'll pay the charges."

"No problem," Jim Bob said, "just don't leave it talking."

"Thanks." I turned to Russel. "I'm just on a tear. I miss my family."

"Understood," Russel said.

I went upstairs. The phone was on a little end table on the landing and there was a chair there. I sat down and called home. On the third ring Ann answered. I realized from her voice, which sounded as if it were coming from underwater, that she had already gone to sleep. I looked at my watch. It was later than I thought, and she always had been the early to bed, early to rise type. "Hi," I said. "It's me."

"Richard?"

"No, your other husband."

"Huh?"

"Yeah, it's me. How you doing baby?"

"Good...what time is it?"

"About ten-thirty. I forgot you'd be in bed. I wasn't thinking about the time."

"Everything okay?"

"Yeah."

"I'm real tired, honey. I got to go to work in the morning."

That Ann, what a romantic.

"Yeah, well.... I'm sorry. I just wanted to call and say I love you."

"No, it's okay. I'm just tired is all. I love you too."

"How's Jordan."

"In bed."

"He okay?"

"Uh huh. You sound funny, Richard."

"Connection. I'm tired myself. Ann?"

"Uh huh?"

"Do you think Jordan loves me?"

"Of course. You know he does."

"I mean, do you think I'm a good father?"

"Yeah. You're impatient and loud sometimes, but you're a good father. You're a good husband too. Especially when you let me sleep."

I almost laughed, but couldn't quite manage it.

"Will you tell him I love him?"

"Uh huh."

"First thing in the morning, will you tell him that?"

"I will."

"You won't forget."

"No, I won't forget.... Are you sure you're okay, Richard?"

"I'm fine."

"Call me tomorrow. Things are kind of fuzzy. I don't wake up too fast."

"I know. I shouldn't have called."

"No, hey, it's okay."

"I love you."

"I love you too."

"Don't forget to tell Jordan."

"I won't. When are you coming home? We miss you."

"Real soon."

"Make it sooner than that."

"I'll try. Good night, honey."

"Good night, Richard."

32.

I awoke to Jim Bob shaking me.

"Get up," he said. "I can't sleep."

"What if I could have?"

"You'd have been shit out of luck. Were you sleeping?"

"I was doing a pretty good imitation of it."

"I keep thinking...you know."

"The video," I said.

"Yeah, that and Russel."

I shifted and sat up on the side of the bed. Jim Bob sat down in a chair by the window and pulled back the curtain and looked out. Moonlight fell on his face like a silver blade. He looked different without his hat, sitting there in a chair in his underwear.

He dropped the curtain and turned to look at me, his face mostly in shadow now. "That bastard out there has been a friend of mine a long time."

"You haven't seen him in nearly twenty years."

"That doesn't matter. We practically grew up together. I thought about him there in the pen, thought about him a lot. I tried to stay in touch with him, but he cut me off. He cut his wife and Freddy off.... Shit, you think him not being around Freddy could have made the kid that way?"

"I don't know. It's hard to believe anything could make somebody like that. You got to think they were born that way. Something missing. Even Russel says he's missing something himself. Has a hole in him and his soul is seeping out of it."

"That sounds like him," Jim Bob said. "He's not as bad as he puts it."

"He's not like Freddy, that's for sure. If he's missing something, he knows it and he's trying to get it back."

"You called your wife?"

"Yeah. I'll give you some money for the call."

"That's all right. How was she?"

"Fine."

"The boy?"

"Fine."

"You're a lucky man, Dane. Got a family. Someone to care about you. I got what I do and the Red Bitch—and she's got a dent in it."

"You got pigs."

"Yeah, but every now and then I eat them, so it's hard to form any kind of relationship. I don't think they trust me."

"Jim Bob, what are we going to do?"

"Got any hot ideas?"

"The cops. We give them a tip, send them the tape with an address. Something like that."

"Uh huh, I thought of that. I thought beyond that. While you were sleeping I decided to take some air, and I drove into town to that 7-Eleven where we bought the beer, used their phone booth. Somehow it just seemed right using the phone booth. I called that old ex-sheriff that owes me favors and he called his son for me and his son called me back at the phone booth. I told the son a what-if story about an FBI informant being given a new identity, then getting involved in crime again. It sounded a lot like what we know about Freddy."

He paused to pull back the curtain again and looked out. The moonlight didn't look any better on his face this time.

"And?"

"And, the FBI won't do dick."

"What?"

"They gave him immunity see, and a new identity."

"What's that got to do with it? That was for another deal altogether. This is separate."

"Not the way the feds see it. Isn't that they don't want to nail the bastard, but they see leaving him alone—at least for now—as the lesser of two evils. Least that's my informer's theory on things. He doesn't know the particular case, but he's known others like it. You see, the FBI fixed it for Freddy to be dead, then told him he was safe as a tick in a bear's ass. And though they wouldn't mind coming down on him with both feet and hitting him so hard shit flies out at both ends, they've got their rep to protect."

"Their rep?"

"You see, they did it so it looked like Freddy got himself killed, doing something stupid like burglary. But if it floats to the top that they actually hid his ass, and couldn't keep it hid, other would-be squealers are gonna think it's all an FBI setup. That you don't really get protected at all. You squeal, they go through the motions of giving you a new identity, then bam, they nab you. Maybe on a bum charge later."

"But who would know? He's supposed to be dead."

"No one maybe. But if they bring him in, and the charges start, maybe everyone. They can't take the chance. Once he's arrested or killed, it would be hard to keep who he is a secret a second time. They might be able to do it, but maybe not."

"All right, they hurt a few informers' feelings. So what?"

"Then next time the feds want to snag them a big bunch of bad guys at the expense of saving one of them, and they've got some-one who's thinking of squealing, the squealer might have second thoughts."

"Bullshit," I said. "This is still the United States of America. You just don't let a scumbag like that go."

"Would you like me to give you a flag to wave, or do you just want to sing the national anthem?"

"Bullshit," I said again, only this time more heartfelt.

"Hush," Jim Bob said, "you'll wake up Ben."

"All right," I said, "what if the FBI or someone tips off the Dixie Mafia as to where this guy who double-crossed them is hiding? Wouldn't it be okay if they did the job for the FBI?"

"Then it would look like the FBI can't hide the people they're trying to hide so good."

"They can't. We found him."

"I found him. And I have a contact. And for the most part, my contact knows I'm one of the good guys."

"Couldn't they have inside help too—the Dixie Mafia?"

"Yeah, they could. But I figure if they did they'd already have gotten Freddy. No, I think he's made a clean getaway. And there's another thing. Freddy is most likely killing Mex gals, not Americans. It's not our people dying."

"But they're dying here, in America. Texas, goddamnit."

"Yeah, and it's a crime no matter how you look at it, but the FBI is letting it ride for now. In time they'll take care of him. But it's too soon now."

"What's in time?"

"I don't know. A year maybe. That way they could fix it so it looks like an accident or something. But if anything happens now, it makes the FBI look bad."

"This is nuts. The FBI doesn't want to look bad, so they're letting this psycho kill women and make videos of it?"

"They're looking at the big picture, and we're looking at the smaller picture."

"Ask those dead women how small the picture is."

"I'm not saying I agree with them, Dane, I'm just saying how it is. Look at it like this. The FBI was willing to let you think you killed Freddy Russel to give him a new identity, and they didn't even give you an inkling what was going on. Not even when Ben out there went bug-fuck nutty and came after you. Think of all the grief they caused him. Hell, made him insane. The local cops helped out. I mean the law is like that. They stick together, right or wrong. You wash my dick, I'll wash your dick. The world don't work like *Dragnet* or *Adam-12*. Not when you get down to die dog or eat the hatchet."

"Either the world is getting more complicated, or I'm just now starting to see things as they are."

"A little of both."

"This connection with the FBI, he didn't have anything else to say?"

"He said my favors with his dad were all used up."

"That's it? No suggestions?"

"Just one. And I didn't like it much."

"Well?"

"He said we could take care of the bastard ourselves."

33.

We talked a while longer and decided on nothing. All the choices sucked. Jim Bob finally gave it up and went upstairs to try and sleep some. I tried to go back to sleep, but lay there looking at the ceiling. I thought about how nuts things were. About how just a little while ago I was a pretty happy guy who was unsure of just a few things, and a little worried about what kind of father I was. And how now I was a very unhappy guy unsure of many things, and even more concerned about what kind of father I was, because nothing in the world looked easy or sure, and everything in the world had to do with being a father. Everything.

I lay there thinking about Russel out there, sleeping now, not knowing what we knew, trying to find some courage in his heart to go and talk to his only son and tell him he loved him.

"Hi, son, I love you."

"Hi, dad. I make movies. I kill girls and get it on video."

It was all very sick and very sad, and it made me think my dad had seen something in the world I hadn't seen, shadows perhaps, those waltzing shadows Russel had talked about, and the shadows were not something he could live with, so he had taken a gun and put it in his mouth and pulled the trigger and sent the shadows away. He didn't have to face them anymore. All his troubles had gone bye-bye. He didn't have to worry about his honor. About being a coward. The nature of the universe. The price of beer and peanuts and where this month's rent or house payment was coming from.

Across all the years of my life I had dreamed of many things. Of toys and then bigger toys and a woman to love and a houseful of kids and a life like *Father Knows Best*, and maybe to be rich and respected and to have plenty of time on my hands and to like that time. But here I was with just a few hours before morning, and they were horrid hours, and it was as if I had more time than ever these days, and so much of it was there to kill, not to enjoy, and that thought depressed me more. And on the other side of those hours were more hours and I had a fear that after the next few days there would be even longer hours full of those goddamn waltzing shadows.

I told myself I wouldn't sleep, and to hell with it.

But finally I closed my eyes and it was morning, and I got up and put on my clothes and went into the living room.

Russel was at the table, drinking coffee, and Jim Bob was standing over in the kitchen looking out the window at the pig house or the garden or nothing at all. He heard me come in and turned and looked at me. Neither of us could hold the other's eyes. I walked over and got a cup and poured some coffee.

Russel turned around and looked at us. "What's with you fellas? Don't bull me, something's up. It's Freddy, isn't it? You know something you haven't told me."

"I think I fucked up," Jim Bob said. "I don't think this Fred Miller is him after all. I've just been thinking how to tell you, but I don't know how. I don't have any more idea where Freddy is than a goose."

Russel didn't quit staring at us. He pursed his lips and sighed, said, "You're lying to me, Jim Bob."

"Wish I were," Jim Bob said. "It's embarrassing to be wrong, and I hate it for you, but—"

"How do you suddenly know you're wrong?"

"The Mexican at the house."

"You could have come up with better than that," Russel said. "That doesn't mean a thing. That guy wasn't Fred Miller. He was a Mexican, like you said. I read a Mexican name off the inside of his wallet."

"Yeah, but—"

"Tell me," Russel said. "Even when I said you might have screwed up earlier, I didn't really think so. It was just something to say. I've known you a long time, and even if I haven't seen you in twenty years, it's just like it was yesterday. You haven't changed a bit. You're still the same egotistical bastard you always were. And you're too good at what you do. You know it, and I know it. And what about you, Dane? What's your story?"

I wanted a smooth lie to come out, but nothing did. I just stood there holding my cup of coffee, not quite looking at Russel.

"If he's dead, tell me. The worse thing that could happen to me is not to know what's happened to him. You know something, I want to know it."

"All right," Jim Bob said. "But there's worse things than being dead."

"Just tell me."

Jim Bob put his coffee cup down and went out of the room and came back with the video. He held it out from him, as if it could bite. He went over to the television and turned it on and put the cassette in the machine.

"What are you doing?" Russel said. "We're talking about Freddy. I don't want to see a movie."

"This will answer your questions," Jim Bob said. "Don't say I didn't warn you. Dane, come on."

He turned on the machine and started walking toward the front door. I went after him, carrying my coffee cup with me.

"Hey," Russel said.

"The answer's on the cassette," I said.

Jim Bob and I went outside. We stood around on the front lawn looking out at the blacktop, neither of us saying anything.

There was an oak in the yard near the road, and I focused my attention on a blackbird in that. It kept hopping from one limb to another, working itself down. It looked weak and sick. It was missing a lot of feathers. Maybe someone had taken a shot at it.

An old pickup rattled by and the old black man driving it waved at us and we waved back.

I looked back to the oak and my bird, but it had flown, or maybe gotten behind some of the thicker branches.

I looked at my watch but didn't really notice the time.

I finished off my coffee and let the cup dangle from my finger like an oversized ring.

It was starting to get hot already, and the coffee I had drunk and my nerves weren't helping matters. My shirt felt sticky beneath my arms.

The front door opened.

Russel came out walking very fast. He went directly toward Jim Bob.

"Ben," Jim Bob said.

Ben looped the punch. It wasn't one of his wise ones. It was worse than the kind he'd told me not to throw. It caught the wind and made it whistle. Jim Bob could have ducked it. Hell, he could have walked to town and caught a bus before it came around.

But he didn't. He closed his eyes the moment before impact and Russel's fist caught him just above the ear and staggered him. Then Ben's other first came around and hit Jim Bob on the side of the jaw and Jim Bob fell to his knees.

Russel turned on me, cocked back his hand. I just stood there and let him come. Like Jim Bob, I wanted to take it. Cleanse myself with pain.

But he didn't hit me. The steam had gone out of him. He

dropped his hand and staggered. I caught him and he hung onto me and hugged me and started to cry and call me a sonofabitch. He heaved so hard I thought his chest would crack my sternum. "It was him, wasn't it?" he said. "It was really Freddy, wasn't it?"

"It was him," I said.

"You sonofabitches. Both you sonofabitches."

Jim Bob came over and put his arms around both of us.

"I'm sorry, Ben," Jim Bob said. "I'm sorrier than I've ever been."

"Jesus, Jesus," Russel said. "My son, my son."

He melted down then, and I got his shoulders and Jim Bob got his feet and we carried him inside and put him on the couch. The television was still on and the tape was still playing, but there wasn't any picture, just static. I cut off the machine and turned off the television. Jim Bob sat on the couch with Russel and held his hand like a little boy.

I went back outside and saw that I had dropped my coffee cup in the grass. I picked it up and went over to the oak and leaned on it, trying to draw some strength from the big old thing, but it wasn't working. I felt weaker than ever.

When I looked down, I saw what had become of my blackbird. It lay dead next to the trunk of the oak, its beak open as if the fall had taken it by surprise.

34.

While Russel lay in a sort of stupor on the couch and Jim Bob sat by him, I got a beer and went out back and walked down to the hog house. Raoul, a stringy man with oversized clothes and a straw hat that looked as if it had gone through a fan, was there. I had seen him from a distance a couple of times, but had never spoken to him. He would come and go like a ghost, leaving garden and hogs attended to.

I went out there and found a lawn chair by the hog house and watched Raoul go about his paces of turning on the irrigation system Jim Bob had devised, and then going into the hog house to do whatever he did there.

He looked at me suspiciously a few times, but if he thought I didn't belong, he kept it to himself. When he was finished, he gave me a kind of shy wave, and I waved back. He got in a pickup with one door tied on with baling wire and drove off leaving at least a quart of K-Mart's cheapest oil transformed into a dark, poisonous cloud behind him.

I sat there with an empty beer bottle and blew air into it, trying to strike up a jug band tune without any success. A blue bottle fly big enough to need air clearance flew around my head a few times and I swatted at him with the bottle, but he got away. He was big, but quick. I finally quit blowing in the bottle and the fly didn't come back. It was getting hot. I felt paralyzed. Sweat ran down my face and into my collar. I wondered what the weather was like on Maui.

Then Jim Bob called to me, "Come on in the house, Dane."

I didn't want to, but I did. When I stepped inside, Russel was at the table and he had a bottle of Jim Beam, and a little glass. I hadn't seen the whiskey before, and figured Jim Bob had brought it out. Russel looked at me and tried to smile, but the muscles in his mouth weren't cooperating.

"Ben wants to say something," Jim Bob said. "Sit down, would you?"

I went over to the couch and sat. Jim Bob poured some of the Jim Beam in a little glass and brought it over to me. I hated the stuff, but I sipped at it anyway. I would have drunk cherry dog piss right then. I felt as if I had been hit with a mallet. It could have been the beer on an empty stomach, and it could have been poor Russel or the video. All those things most likely.

"Freddy," Russel said in an uncharacteristically low voice, "is out of control. An understatement. He's off the end. He's my son, and I feel responsible."

"You're not responsible," I said.

"Shut up...please," Russel said. "I feel responsible. He's flesh of my flesh, blood of my blood, and all that shit. But he's no good. There's nothing about that boy worth saving. He's not a petty criminal, he's the dredge at the bottom of the sewer."

A tear ran out of Russel's right eye and went down his face quick as a bullet and gathered in the bristle of whiskers on his cheek. He tossed off his whiskey and poured himself another.

I looked at Jim Bob. He looked very old. He was leaning against the bar holding a glass of whiskey and he was looking at Russel, and he looked like he might cry at any moment.

I drank some of my whiskey. I wished I hadn't. It was hot and nasty, but I sipped it again. It was something to keep my hands from flying around.

"I think when a man has lost the things that make him a man," Russel said. "Then he doesn't need to live. Jim Bob says the law would be reluctant to do it. I don't understand that. I'm a god-damn thief and I don't understand that. If the law won't do it, I have to."

"You can't do that," I said. "He's your son."

"That's why I have to do it. I brought him into this world, and now, I have to take him out of it. It's the only thing I can do for him as a father. He might not know it, but it's a goddamn gift. Shit, he's dead already."

"You could hire someone," I said

"No," Russel said.

"I offered to do it," Jim Bob said.

"No, I've got to do this thing."

"You do," I said, "and you won't be able to live with yourself."

"I can't live with myself now. Not knowing this."

We sat there in silence and sipped our whiskey. A clock ticked somewhere and there was a hum I hadn't noticed before. Probably the refrigerator.

"What is it you want to do, Ben?" Jim Bob said. "I mean, how?"

"I don't know yet," Russel said. "Just walk up and do it, I guess."

"There's the big Mex," Jim Bob said, "he might be with Freddy."

"I guess I'll shoot him too," Russel said.

"Might not be that easy," Jim Bob said.

Russel looked at Jim Bob. "You trying to count yourself in?"

"Yeah," Jim Bob said. "Backup. Help you scope things out. If you're going to do it, I want you to come out of it alive and away from the law. They might not want to come down on Freddy, but they would you. You'd end up making them look bad. It'll be said the FBI can't take care of their charges, or that they're double-crossers. They won't like that, and they'll clobber you but good."

"You know you could get your ass shot off," Russel said.

"I know," Jim Bob said. "I'm not an ignoramus. But I won't get my ass shot off. I'm fucking immortal."

Slowly they turned their attention to me.

"I don't know," I said. "I got a family."

"And a good one," Russel said. "Go back to them and take care of them. This isn't a thing for you, and I wouldn't want it to be. Something were to happen to you, and I'd have it on my head from here on out. Things are bad enough without me adding that."

"I think maybe if I didn't have a family—"

"You don't need to explain yourself," Jim Bob said. "We won't think the worse of you."

"And what if we did?" Russel said. "We're just a thief and a hog-raising private eye."

"You're sure this is something you want to do?" I asked Russel.

"It's the first thing I've ever been sure of in my life," Russel said. "Bad as it is."

Jim Bob came over and poured me some more whiskey I didn't want, poured Russel and himself another.

"What I'll do," I said, "is stay with you guys until you've looked things over, seen how it's to be done. You might need me for something. When it comes time for...when it's time, take me to the bus station."

"Fair enough," Russel said. "And thanks."

35.

"This here," Jim Bob said introducing us to the man, "is Manuel Rodriguez. He's in the country legal, but he ain't a legal doctor."

"That was a nice introduction," Rodriguez said shaking our hands, "I hope to do the same for you another time, Jim Bob."

"Important here everyone knows how we stand," Jim Bob said.

"Ah, business," Rodriguez said. He was a little guy, maybe four feet eight with black hair going gray at the temples. His eyes threatened to close even as he looked at you, as if he had been awake too long. He had some ill-fitting dentures, and I kept wanting to hold my hand under his chin lest they fall out while he talked. We were at his house. A hot little wood-frame place he shared with Raoul, three other women and a little girl. The place smelled of sweat and cabbage, and mildew that came from the old straw that backed the almost worthless water fan in the living room window. Two of the women looked to be in their thirties, the other, perhaps Rodriguez's wife, was closer to fifty. They all wore clothes that were too small or too large. Jeans and blouses and flat-heeled shoes fresh from garage sales. The little girl wore a stained yellow dress and had a doll without any clothes. She sat on the floor and looked at me. I smiled at her. She smiled back, but she didn't come over to see me.

Jim Bob had brought meat and vegetables with him, and he gave those to the older woman and she thanked him in Spanish and gave him a nod. He said something back to her, and she took the meat and put it in the freezer compartment of a bullet-shaped refrigerator and put the tomatoes in the bottom. She took the okra to the sink and started washing it. One of the younger women got a pan out from under the sink and set it on the drainboard and the younger woman took a knife and cut the okra up and put it in the pan. The third woman stood by, as if on sentry duty. She had a stern face, like she had seen much and hadn't liked any of it. I wondered if this was Raoul's wife, the one whose pussy hair he didn't want to plant. Raoul himself, after a friendly greeting, had gone outside.

No one introduced us to the women.

We sat on the couch for a time, and Jim Bob and Rodriguez talked about the weather and Jim Bob told him about his hogs. The third woman, the one that might have been Raoul's wife, seemed to be taking a personal interest in me, and like the things she had seen before, I wasn't any better. I smiled at her, but she didn't smile back. I checked my fly casually. Zipped. She finally quit watching me and left the room, no doubt to glare at some wallpaper or something. The little girl held up her doll for me to see, but it was a look from a distance. She still didn't come over to see me. I smiled at her and she kept smiling. The two women at the sink kept their backs to us. Russel got up and went out on the front porch to smoke a cigarette. I twiddled my thumbs and tried to look interested in the conversation, which had switched from hogs to the Astros. Jim Bob and Rodriguez were worried about someone's pitching arm. I wished I had a cigarette to smoke.

"Shall we go outside, gentlemen?" Rodriguez said.

"Why the hell not," Jim Bob said, and we all went out to join

Russel on the front porch. I smiled at the little girl on the way out and patted her doll on the head when she held it up to me.

It was cooler on the porch than inside. There was an old couch on the porch, and Rodriguez sat on that. Jim Bob sat down on the edge of the porch and Russel sat down on the steps. That left me to lean on the porch post, because the rest of the couch was a disaster area. Springs stuck up through the cushions like corkscrews craving your ass.

Rodriguez's manner had changed now that we were outside. He looked a little more alert. "The money up front like last time?" he said going right into it.

"Five hundred up front," Jim Bob said, "and if nothing happens, you keep it. We get some holes in us, I'll pay you whatever it takes to plug them."

"Last time," Rodriguez said, "it was five hundred just for you."

"It's five hundred for all of us this time," Jim Bob said. "You have to work on more than one of us, I'll pay you for what it's worth. You know my word is good."

"Medicine, when you are not legal, is very expensive," Rodriguez said, looking pained by the fact.

"I know that. Wouldn't need you if you were legal. We just want to make sure we got someone here to take care of us so we won't have to report any bullet wounds to the police."

"I can only do so much. If it's real bad—"

"We go through this every time," Jim Bob said.

"I like you to know," Rodriguez said, and he waved a hand at us. "I want them to know. I can only do so much without a hospital and nurses and the good medicines."

"They understand," Jim Bob said.

Rodriguez considered. "Five hundred for three up front is not much."

"Take it or go fuck a goat," Jim Bob said.

Rodriguez smiled and his false teeth looked certain to go for a dive. I started to leap for them, but by some miracle they stayed in his mouth. "I like goats," he said. "They feel good and tight on the dick and they don't talk back and want to have this orgasm thing. They just *baa* a little. But you see, I got the wife. And she does talk. She likes money. We have to pay the rent on this very nice place. She and I are legal, but the others are not. They work hard to pay their part of the rent, but they can't get very good jobs—"

"I pay Raoul good," Jim Bob said with more than a taste of indignation.

"And my wife and I, we're not making so much either. Ever since the legal abortions, I've hardly made enough to put food on the table. And Rosalita, she has the bad knees. And there's the little girl—"

"Christ," Jim Bob said, "all right, all right cut the fucking fiddle music."

"But I haven't told you about the old mother I send money to in Mexico."

"Good," Jim Bob said. "Don't. I'll make it a thousand up front, just to have you on hold, but that's more than you're worth. I'm doing this for your wife, who deserves an orgasm, by the way, and Raoul's little girl. To hell with your old mother in Mexico. She's probably been dead fifteen years."

"Twenty," Rodriguez said.

Jim Bob sighed like Atlas's job with the world had just been handed to him. He got up and took out his wallet and turned slightly so Rodriguez couldn't see in it. He took out some bills. He put the wallet in his back pocket again and went over to Rodriguez and bent down and placed the bills separate of each other along the Mexican's leg and straightened up.

"Count 'em," Jim Bob said.

Rodriguez did. "Very good," he said. "A thousand. I am now on duty."

"Just make sure you don't go to Mexico anytime soon to see your old mother's grave."

Rodriguez laughed and showed those ill-fitting false teeth again.

Damn, those things made me nervous. "I will be here until you tell me this thing is done and you do or do not need me."

"Another thing," Jim Bob said. "We'll need to borrow a car for a day or two. Three at the most."

"You are welcome to Raoul's truck," Rodriguez said.

"That's generous of you with his truck," Jim Bob said, "but I really didn't want to send up a smoke signal everywhere I went. Something with four doors would be nice. Inconspicuous, unlike the Bitch. And since you only have one other car, I must be talking about that one."

"You must be," Rodriguez said. "That would be the Rambler, of course."

"Very good," Jim Bob said.

Rodriguez shook his head. "The car is a great comfort to me. I have places to go, people to see, things to do."

"How much?" Jim Bob said.

"About forty dollars a day," Rodriguez said.

"Forty dollars a day," Jim Bob said. "I can rent cheaper than that from fucking Hertz. I'll give you twenty dollars flat out for as long as I need it. I'll check the oil and water and bring it back with a full tank."

"Very well," Raoul said. 'Twenty dollars for as long as you need it."

Jim Bob looked suspicious. "That was too easy."

Rodriguez shrugged. "It has three flats."

36.

When we got back from town with three new tires for the Rambler, Jim Bob said to me: "From here on out, you're not paying anything. This is mine and Russel's show, and I'll put up the gravy. I got enough saved to do us just fine. You stay along for as long as you like, then cut out when you want."

The Rambler was out back of Rodriguez's house, parked in a little shed that had once held chickens and still held their calling cards: dirty feathers and dried chicken manure. When you walked in there, the smallest feathers and the dust rose up in a fine, dry cloud and tried to make residence in your nose and throat and choke you to death. The shed being constructed mostly of tin made it as hot as a lion's balls in the Congo.

The Rambler looked sad there on its three flat tires and the one with tread so thin you could damn near see air through it. There was a coat of dust on it thick enough to plant turnips.

Jim Bob got the jack, tire tool and four-way tool out of the trunk, jacked up the front of the Rambler while Russel quickly loosened the bolts. Rodriguez came out to smile at us with his bad dentures.

"Good tires?" Rodriguez said.

"Best Sears sells," Jim Bob said. "Would I jack you on tires?"

"You might do that," Rodriguez said.

"They got tread on them and they hold air," Jim Bob said, "and that's a sight more than I can say for these dudes. Now run along and play and let us work."

"Make the bolts tight," Rodriguez said, and walked off.

When he was out of earshot, Russel said, "Can he be trusted?"

"Wouldn't have brought him in on this if I didn't think he could," Jim Bob. said. "I've used him before, couple of times. Didn't need him either time, but I was kind of comforted knowing he was there."

"Yeah," Russel said, "but we get hit we got to get to him in time."

"Be an optimist," Jim Bob said. "I am. Gets you through life happier than a lizard."

"What about guns?" Russel asked.

"I got us covered on that."

"When I shoot Freddy," Russel said softly, "I don't want it to.... I want something that will take him out. You know what I mean. I don't want him to suffer. Just bam and it's over."

"It's how you use what you have," Jim Bob said, "but I'll try and get something with some punch. I've got a .357. That could be the thing. I also got the sawed-off and an Ithaca 12-gauge."

"I don't like the idea of a shotgun somehow," Russel said. "It seems...messy."

"It is messy," Jim Bob said. "It's all messy.... Look, you want to back out of this plan, suits me."

"You back out," Russel said, "and I'll still go through with it, one way or another."

"All right," Jim Bob said. "I'll get you something that's a stopper. It'll be up to you to put the bullet home."

"I used to be able to shoot," Russel said. He took off the old tire and I rolled the new, mounted one around to him and he put it on the wheel stubs and put on the lug bolts and Jim Bob let the jack down. Russel tightened the lug bolts, and we went around back to replace the other two.

When we were finished, Russel stood up and wiped his hands on his pants and said, "I want him to know who I am, and what I'm doing," he said. "But I don't want him to hurt much. I want it to be quick. That's why I want the right gun, Jim Bob. You know what I'm saying?"

"I know," Jim Bob said.

I drove the Rambler and Jim Bob and Russel went in the pickup. At the house, Jim Bob seated us at the kitchen table and gave us beers, then went upstairs and came back down carrying pistols.

He put one of the revolvers on the table.

"A .38, short-barreled, no sight. A belly gun. I thought I'd use it and the sawed-off double-barrel I got in the Bitch's trunk. That way I'll have some insurance should the Mexican get into things. I got a hunch both those boys carry guns."

"The .357 is for me?" Russel said.

"Yeah." Jim Bob reached in his shirt pocket and took out a little plastic case and put it and the .357 on the table next to the .38. "There's your ammunition," he said. "I've got a speed loader for you and a holster. You might want to wear one of my sport jackets so you can keep it out of sight."

"Sport jacket?" I said.

"Well, I don't wear it much," Jim Bob said. "It ain't my style."

"I can believe that," I said.

"I guess we're set," Russel said, looking at the gun as if someone had shit a turd in the middle of the table.

"I've got a snub-nose .38 in the trunk of the Bitch with an ankle holster. You can wear that for backup."

"That's all right," Russel said.

"I'm not asking, I'm saying. I'm still running the show here, and I say you wear the ankle holster. None of this suits you, I got a couple more guns upstairs, .45 automatic, a .44 Western style revolver and an Ithaca 12-gauge. All this is cold stuff, by the way. No way it can be traced unless we get sloppy and leave them lying around with our fingerprints on them."

"Or they find your bodies," I said. "Have you thought of that? They just might outshoot you."

"I've thought I might get wounded," Jim Bob said, "and that's as far as I've thought. I won't let myself think beyond that. Last two times I didn't even get that. Came out without a scratch."

"Was there shooting?"

"First time I bluffed. Second time there was shooting. I shot a little faster."

"What now?" Russel said. "What's our next step?"

"We leave the guns for now and start checking Freddy out," Jim Bob said. "Follow him around for a few days. Find out where he goes and when, and figure how hard or how easy this is all going to be. We get his program down, then we make our own program. Then we do it." Jim Bob turned to me. "I got the Rambler so if we needed a backup car, something less conspicuous than the Red Bitch, we'd have it. Ben and I'll do the first watch in the truck. We find out anything that needs you and the Rambler, I'll call you here. We may just want to switch cars so they won't be seeing the same one all the time and get suspicious. Guess that's all you need to know for now."

"All right," I said.

"Before you say that," Jim Bob said, "understand exactly what you're into. You're helping plot a murder. We're going to kill a man and you are an accessory to the deed. You don't get caught, you got to go through life living with it. Think you can?"

"I don't like the idea," I said, "but if I went away now I'd still know you were going to do it, and my knowing is just as bad. I'm going to end up living with it one way or another."

"I just want it understood," Russel said, "that when it comes to Freddy, I do the shooting, Jim Bob."

"No promises," Jim Bob said. "Looks like Freddy is going to give me a ventilator shaft, I'm taking him out. I'll do my best to do it your way, but I'm not putting my head on the block. I don't go that far for anyone. Thing is we're going to do it, and that's enough."

"When do we start?" I asked.

"Tomorrow morning," Jim Bob said. "Early."

37.

Next morning, well before light, Jim Bob and Russel drove away in the pickup. I stayed around the house and killed time. I had an early breakfast of fried eggs and burned toast and too-strong coffee. Later, about eight, I had a muffin and a glass of milk. Before noon I drank a beer. At noon, I ate a sandwich. I had some iced tea. I watched television; about half of a monster movie where irritated puppets were destroying a cardboard city. Where were The Three Stooges when you really needed them?

I was as nervous as a witch during the Inquisition. I wanted to go home. I wanted to see my wife and son. I wanted to go fishing.

I went over and sat by the phone and looked at it.

It wasn't intimidated. It didn't ring. I stopped looking at it. I picked up a magazine about hog raising and read about ear mites in the South; they seemed to be a problem, but nothing that couldn't be defeated. I wondered if Jim Bob's hogs had ear mites. I wondered what the hogs thought about it if they did. I even tried to see the ear mite's side of it.

The phone still didn't ring. It knew I was really watching it out of the corner of my eye. A watched phone never boils, or something like that.

I went upstairs, not to snoop, but because I had to do something. I was about ready to crawl along the wall like Spider-Man. The door to Jim Bob's room was open and I went in there. There was a big table with a computer on it and some computer manuals. There was a row of books next to his bed. The books were all Westerns, Louis L'Amour and T.V. Olsen. There was a shotgun on a deer-antler gun rack over the bed. I went over and tested the tips of the antlers with my finger. Not that sharp. That was all right. I wasn't that sharp either. I was involved in a plot to kill a man I didn't know and had never so much as spoken to. There was already one man dead by my hand, and I didn't even know his name.

On top of the chest of drawers I found a Trojan rubber in its wrapper, some keys, change and a stack of magazines. *Playboy*, *Penthouse*, *Gallery*, and some real sleazoid types. I looked through them. I looked through the sleazoid types a couple of times. Maybe it was three times.

I sang "Home on the Range" and went downstairs.

The phone rang.

It was a siding salesman. I told him no and hung up. I looked at the phone a little while. But not long. I had learned my lesson. I had another beer and went to the bathroom.

The phone rang, of course.

I got my pants snapped and zipped without tearing off any important parts of my person, and answered it on the third ring.

"We'd like one of them pepperoni pizzas, all the goddamn fixings, only cut them little fishes off of it. They make me want to throw up."

"That's funny, Jim Bob."

"Ain't it. Well, we're over here across from The Caravan Video Store, and from the looks of things, Freddy owns it. Maybe the feds set him up with it."

"Would they do that?"

"Oh yeah. They owe him. Don't that take the rag off the bush, though? They take this scumbag and set him up in business and he pretty well does what he wants so the feds don't have to look stupid. You don't see them sonofabitches doing stuff like that for the honest man, do you?"

"He been there all day?"

"Mex came by and got him about six-thirty this morning, drove him to work, and even drove him to the Pizza Hut for lunch. You know, they done got the dents out of that Chevy Nova."

"That's all you found out?"

"He likes pepperoni pizza."

"Great."

"What's to find out in one day? I doubt there's going to be that many astounding revelations anyway. Best we can hope for is just get his pattern down and know when to hit him. If we can do it without the Mex around, all the better. Right now it looks like the sonofabitch shares the same pair of shoes with him."

"Yeah, well.... Guess I'm just bored."

"Jack off. That's what I do when I'm bored. It can liven up the dullest of days. Go upstairs and read some of them fuckbooks on my dresser."

"I did."

"They'll put a tire tool in your pants, won't they?"

"I don't want a tire tool in my pants."

"You sound a little bit on the cranky side, Dane. Maybe you ought to have you some milk and cookies, crank the living room air-conditioner to high, stretch out on the couch there and take you a nap. We probably won't need you at all today, so unwind."

"Easier said than done. You're about out of beer by the way. You want some more, you better bring some home."

"What about bread and milk, honey? Do we need that?"

"Ha, ha."

I hung up and went into the kitchen to look for the milk and cookies. I found the milk, but no cookies. I drank the milk, turned the air-conditioner on high and stretched out on the couch for a nap. But it didn't seem right without the cookies.

38.

Next day Jim Bob and I went in the Rambler and Russel stayed home. I pitied him. I hoped he enjoyed reading about ear mites more than I did.

Freddy's schedule was pretty much like it was the day before. We got into Houston and over to the residential area where he lived about six-ten. We parked in the lot of a Safeway store across from where the highway met the street that led out from the sub-division.

At exactly six-thirty-five, the Nova with the Mexican driving came up the street and turned right on the highway. We followed discreetly in the Rambler. There was no air-conditioning in the Rambler, and by seven it was already a little warm. We followed the Nova through some heavy traffic, but Jim Bob never lost sight of it. I noticed that the Nova had all its windows rolled up. Air-conditioning. I liked that. Here we were, the good guys, and we had a hot Rambler. Worse than that, the bad guy had his own driver and a video store somehow provided him by the FBI. It helped with his hobby, which was taking videos of women being fucked and murdered by himself and the Mexican. He probably had all the major credit cards.

The Nova went out of the main of Houston and onto Highway 59 North, and finally came to a section that had once been thick with tits-and-ass joints, but was now only a few topless lounges and cheap eateries, mobile homes and used car lots. And a video store called The Caravan.

The Nova turned right off of 59 and went around back of the video place. The store was tucked neatly between an outdoor motor sales and a garage that had a sign that said it specialized in foreign cars and transmission work. It was seven-thirty sharp.

We drove on past a ways, then Jim Bob turned around and we pulled off an annex road and found a little truck stop and had breakfast. When that was finished, we went to a used car lot that was catercorner and across the highway from The Caravan and walked around the lot looking at cars and kicking tires and keeping a sideways view on the video store. A plump salesman with white hair slicked back, wearing a plaid sports coat, maroon tie, lime green slacks and white shoes, tried to tell us why a used car was ten times better than a new one.

Jim Bob had him show us all the cars on the highway side of the lot, and we looked at them real slow and asked technical questions and took turns sitting behind the wheel of each and every one of them. The salesman's smile had almost fallen down his throat and he was beginning to look a little woozy from the heat. His cheap plaid sports coat had wells of sweat under the arms and there was a ring of it around his neck and a splotch under the knot of his tie.

"Confidentially, Horace," Jim Bob said, having latched onto the man's name, "I don't think I could buy a car I hadn't driven."

"Course not," said Horace.

"We'd like to test-drive a few of these babies. See how they respond. We'll start with this Skylark, if that's all right."

"By all means," Horace said producing a monogrammed, green hanky and wiping his face. "We here at Horace Williams's Motors aim to please. That's our motto, and we live by it."

"And it's a good motto," Jim Bob said. "A business that don't care about its customers is no business at all. That's what I always say, don't I?"

"Yes," I said, "you always say that."

"I'll get the keys," Horace said.

We drove the air-conditioned Skylark around a bit, going by the video store now and then, never getting too far away from it.

We swapped that car for a red '68 Chevy, with air-conditioning, and drove it around, this time actually crossing over to the video store and driving back between the outdoor motor place and going around back. We saw the Nova parked there next to a gray Vette.

Jim Bob turned us around and we went back to the used car dealer. After about five cars, Horace didn't look nearly so ready to please. He even told us he thought old Ramblers were pretty good cars, and how if he had one, he might hang onto it.

"Guess you're right," Jim Bob said. "But we'll be back tomorrow to look at the rest of them. I think if you'd had that Skylark in metal flake blue we'd have had a deal."

There was a filling station almost directly across from The Caravan, and that was our next stop. Jim Bob shook hands with the owner of the station. He knew him from the day before.

"This is Phil," Jim Bob said introducing the station owner to me. He didn't bother to give my name to Phil.

"New man, Phil. I'm supposed to break him in today."

"Well, I don't envy you men any," Phil said. "Hot work sitting out there in a car."

"Ain't that the truth," Jim Bob said, and gave him a smile.

"Come on," he said to me. "Let's get to work."

The car was parked next to a telephone booth and it was pointing in the direction of the video store. We got in it and I said, "Exactly what is our work, Jim Bob?"

"Highway Department. We're supposed to count how many tractor-trailer trucks come by here in a given hour."

"Any reason?"

"Road damage. Gives some clue to the wear and tear on the road. Big trucks like that are hard on the concrete. You count about three hours a day, for a few days, and you can get some kind of idea as to what kind of beating the highway's taking. You can average that out and make plans for when to have the road repaired. That way you don't wait until it's in awful shape and there's craters out there big enough to lose a Volkswagen in, though it wouldn't hurt my feelings if all them foreign sonofabitches fell off in a hole. I think you should buy American."

"Where did you learn all that, Jim Bob?"

"I made it up yesterday."

We stayed there a couple of hours, and it got bloody hot. I felt as if my brain was boiling and about to run out my ears. Jim Bob told some jokes that weren't any good and we sang "The Great Speckled Bird" together. We weren't half-bad. We did every television theme song we knew and we even hummed some hymns.

Finally I didn't want to sing anymore. Jim Bob got a magazine out of the backseat and read it and eyeballed the video store over it from time to time. It was one of those hog-raising magazines. I wondered if it had an article on ear mites too.

The Caravan did a brisk trade. People went in and out all day, renting and perhaps buying videos. A couple of times I wondered if maybe someone had gone in there to buy a snuff film, but ruled that out. That was too easy. Those things would be sold to special people in special places, for big money.

And maybe not. Maybe if the right person had the money, they could get it across the counter. One Porky's, a Bugs Bunny Cartoon, and oh yeah, your latest snuff film.

Jim Bob gave me the magazine. I thumbed through it. There were some good photographs of hogs.

"Here's one I bet you don't know," Jim Bob said, and he began to hum the theme to *Secret Agent Man.*

"*Secret Agent Man*, and shut up."

About eleven-fifteen the Nova came around the corner with the Mex driving and Freddy on the front passenger side.

"Lunchtime," Jim Bob said, and started the Rambler. We followed them to the Pizza Hut and cruised on by.

"Creatures of habit," I said.

"Yeah," Jim Bob said. "Let's go down here and get a burger and see if we can pick them back up at the store. I have a feeling they keep a pretty regular schedule. Man, how would you like to eat pizza every day?"

"Thing that gets me," I said, "is they're so normal acting. They go to work and eat pizza, and murder women. Do you think they'll do it again?"

"I think they'll do it until we put a stop to it. If they'd done it only once, that would be enough for me. I'd as soon the law come down on them, but since they, won't, it's up to me and Russel."

We got a greasy burger and a Coke and took our time. When we were finished, we went back to the station and bought a couple of Cokes from the machine inside and sat out in the Rambler, our home away from home, and sipped them. My Coke turned hot before I was halfway finished with it, and I opened the door and poured it out. I got bored enough to actually count the tractor-trailer trucks that went by; Jim Bob's theory had come to make a certain type of sense to me. It was that hot.

About three I opened the door and threw up my hot Coke. Jim Bob went in the station and bought me some peanut butter crackers and a Sprite. "Here," he said, "this will go well with an upset stomach."

I doubted it, but I nibbled on a cracker and sipped the Sprite. I began to envy Russel at home in the air-conditioning. Nothing to do but watch monster movies and look at girly magazines and read about ear mites.

"It's the glamour that keeps me in this kind of work," Jim Bob said. "Good hours and scenery. Chance to meet fascinating people, and of course there's the retirement plan."

At four o'clock, the Nova came out from behind The Caravan. The Mexican was the only one on board. Jim Bob cranked up the Rambler and we found a lull in traffic and drove on across to the video store parking lot.

"Just the Mex has seen us, so you go in and have a look around. Get the lay of the land. This may be where we do it."

"Here?"

"It's either here or the house," Jim Bob said. "If the Mex comes back, I'll start honking my horn like I'm out here waiting on you and I'm impatient. Note the back door, anything like that."

Inside there were rows and rows of videos. There was a little thin guy behind the counter. He was wearing a white suit that looked ten years old. It had gone slightly yellow, and was more yellow still under the arms. He had on a white shirt with it and no tie. He needed a shave.

There wasn't much to see. The usual videos. No section for snuff films. I was about to leave, when a door opened at the back behind the counter, and Freddy came out. I felt tension beating its wings in my stomach.

He had on a very expensive gray suit and it was cut to hide his belly and it did the job well. He had on a gray tie with little blue stripes in it and there was some kind of gold designed tie tack stuck through it and into his dark shirt. I bet his shoes were shiny. He and Price could have competed for best dressed.

I couldn't help myself. I went over to the counter and looked right at Freddy. I said, "Have you got *Murmur of the Heart*? It's a French film."

"We don't carry nothing foreign but the Jap and Mex stuff," the skinny guy answered for him. "People go for the Jap stuff. Lots of action, all that swords and kicking and jumping stuff."

Freddy smiled at me, and damned if it wasn't a nice smile. He was a nice looking guy when he wasn't raping and killing someone. It gave me a chill. He looked so normal. The kind of guy that might coach your kid in football or teach social studies. "That's right, mister," he said. "Only Japanese and Mexican films. The rest are American and maybe some British."

"We got Limey films?" the thin guy said.

Freddy looked at him and smiled. It was, as I said, a nice smile, but I could recall seeing it on his face the moment before he shot that girl and licked her blood from the wound. "These are modern times," Freddy said to the thin guy. "I'd prefer you not use offensive terms like Jap and Limey if you're going to work for me. Okay?"

"Sure," the thin man said. "I didn't mean nothing by it, really." He seemed desperate to convince.

"I'm sure you didn't," Freddy said, "but I'd prefer not to hear those kind of racist remarks in my presence, customers or no customers."

Freddy smiled at me, and I found I couldn't quit staring. I was looking for some sign of the beast, something that would alert me to his madness or meanness, or whatever you call the bile in a man like Freddy, but all I saw was a regular human being. He wasn't the sort of guy the movies would pick to play the kind of guy he was; he was more the kind to be typecast as a film hero's best buddy.

"Well, thanks anyway," I said.

"Maybe next time," Freddy said. "We intend to expand our line."

I nodded and started out, and even though the air-conditioning in there worked quite well, before I could get outside, sweat beads had formed on my forehead and my palms had turned sticky.

We got our place back at the station, and about fifteen minutes later the Mexican returned and parked behind the video store again. He'd probably gone out for a 7-Eleven Slurpee.

At exactly seven o'clock, the video store closed and the Nova drove out, and behind it came the gray Vette with the thin, white-suited man driving it. I could see now that the Vette needed lots of body work. They turned the same direction onto the highway, with the Nova leading, and we fell in behind them, and on the other side of town the Vette honked at the Nova and veered off. The Nova didn't honk back.

We followed the Nova across town and back to Freddy's place. The Mexican was great with traffic. He handled the Chevy like a golf cart, weaving in and out of cars expertly.

They reached the subdivision where Freddy lived at five minutes to eight. We didn't follow them in. We drove on past and turned around and drove home.

39.

When we got back to Jim Bob's place late that evening, Russel met me at the door with, "Your wife called."

"Oh," I said. "What did she say?"

"She didn't want to talk to me, as you can imagine. Wouldn't have, if she hadn't had to. She asked you to call her after five."

It was, of course, well after five then. I said, "Jim Bob, can I drive the Rambler to the store? I'd prefer to use the pay phone."

"Take the truck and use the goddamn air-conditioning. This heat has damn near made me sick. Hell, take the Red Bitch if you want."

"The truck is fine."

I drove over to the store and got some change and called Ann. She answered on the first ring.

"How are you?" she asked.

"I'm fine."

"Come home."

"I can't. Not quite yet."

"You've got to."

"Is Jordan okay?"

"He's fine. It's me that isn't okay. Come home. Quit playing cops and robbers and come home."

"This is serious, Ann."

"All the more reason to come home. Haven't you played this out enough? Who cares who you shot? He had it coming. As for it not being Freddy, that's Russel's problem."

"We've been through this."

"And you've had your fun. Come home."

"Things have changed. It's a lot worse than we thought."

Silence.

"It's seems that Freddy is into some really bad stuff."

"What do you expect from an organized crime informer?"

"Really bad stuff, Ann." And I told her all that we had found out and what Russel and Jim Bob were planning. "And I'm going to help them do it. I thought at first I was just going to go along for part of the ride, but I can't. When I saw Freddy today, I knew I had to go all the way."

"It's not your place to do anything about it."

"Whose place is it? The law? They won't touch him. Not unless he gets totally out of hand, and even then as long as it's Mexicans they won't bother. They want to keep their reputation intact."

"Then let Jim Bob and Russel do it. They want to do it and they know how. You're not a gunfighter."

"I can't just let them do something like that and pretend I'm not part of it because I didn't pull the trigger. I've got to go in there with them, back their play."

"Back their play. Jesus, will you listen to yourself, Richard. Back their play. That's gangster talk."

"Westerns."

"I don't give a damn. It's childish. It's vigilante."

"There's nothing childish about it, unless you want to include the little whore he killed. She was childish. About fifteen, I think. Maybe younger. That's a good age for him. He can trick them easier, less experience. Even if they are whores. And I don't give a fuck if it's vigilante. I'd be glad to let the law do it, but they don't want to."

"Richard. I love you. But I'm not going to sit around here and wonder if you're dead in some ditch somewhere. You come home now, or don't come home. When it's over, if you're okay you tell me, but you don't come home. Ever."

"Ann—"

She hung up.

I drove back to Jim Bob's, my stomach feeling like an empty pot. Maybe, like Russel, there was a hole in me and my soul was oozing out.

But I knew any attempt to talk myself out of what I was planning to do would be useless. This sense of honor I carried was a blind thing. It didn't deal in common sense. It was made up of something I heard my dad say once, one of the few things I truly remembered about him. He said, you do what's right because it's right and you don't need a reason.

Man's got to do what a man's got to do.

I wondered if dad was thinking that way when he put the gun in his mouth.

Man's got to do what a man's got to do.

I got back to Jim Bob's feeling small enough to walk under a snail's belly on stilts, and when I went inside, Jim Bob said, "Your wife's on the phone. She sounds a little distressed. She's been holding for you till you got back."

"Thanks," I said. I started for the phone. Jim Bob reached out and took me by the shoulder.

"Dane, you got a problem at home, you go home and take care of it. This ain't your business. Not really. You're a frame builder from LaBorde, Texas, not a shootist."

"That's what Ann says."

I picked up the phone. "Hello."

"Richard," Ann said, "I think you're a big, dumb, foolish so-nofabitch that's seen too many John Wayne movies and read too many cowboy books, but I'll be waiting. You do what you got to do, damn it. And please, please, be careful and don't get yourself killed. Jordan and I love you."

"I love you too," I said.

When I hung up, I turned to Russel and Jim Bob. "I'm going to need a gun too," I said. "I'm in. All the way."

40.

"Barring some unforeseen circumstance," Jim Bob said, "I'm willing to bet Freddy's routine stays pretty much the same, day in and day out. Off to work at six-thirty-five, back from work just before eight. Except maybe the weekends. But we're not going to wait that long. We're going to do it tomorrow."

It was later that night and we were sitting at Jim Bob's table drinking coffee and eating cookies. He'd had them all along, they were just well hidden.

"I want to give you one more chance to get out, Dane," Jim Bob said.

"Take it," Russel said. "You got what I wish I'd kept. A wife and a son and you're a good father."

"I'm not so sure about the good father part," I said. "I always feel like I'm fucking up."

"Comparing yourself to me," he said, "you're as good a father as they come."

"You had nothing to do with Freddy turning out to be a monster," I said.

"Once he was a little kid playing in the floor with a toy truck,"

Russel said. "He was like any other kid then. There was no monster in him."

"It's all moot now," Jim Bob said. "You in or out, Dane? Now's the time to put your cards on the table. Be sure."

"I said I was in, and I'm in."

"All right. We keep it simple. No hiding out. That would just give us time to be seen by someone. We'll take the truck. I'll put the camper on it, and I've got some putty that looks like mud. I can dab that over the license plates so they can't be made by some alert citizen. I've also got some light blue tape striping, and we'll put that down the sides of the truck. And we'll put a big hood ornament on it. When we get finished, after we do the job, I mean, we'll come back here and get rid of the tape and the putty and the ornament, and we'll take the camper off."

"I know we're going to kill them," I said, "but what's the plan? Do we drive by in the truck and start firing at them?"

"No. That ain't certain enough," Jim Bob said. "When they slow down to go up the little hump that leads into Freddy's driveway, we'll be in motion. We'll pull up at the curb and jump out and shoot at them through the windows. They won't be in a good position to do much fighting back. It's the perfect time."

"And if the windows are rolled up?" I asked.

"Shoot through the windows, Dane," Russel said. "Bullets break glass."

"Oh." Some killer I was. That hadn't occurred to me.

"Thing for us to do now," Jim Bob said, "is go to bed, sleep late, fix up the truck tomorrow and drive over there and wait. And then do it."

That night I dreamed I was standing at one end of a dusty street wearing Roy Rogers garb, lots of fringe and a white hat, and a two-holstered gun belt sporting pearl-handled revolvers. At the other end of the street was Freddy. He was wearing the suit he'd been wearing at the video store. He didn't have a gun belt. The Mexican was off to the side holding his horse for him. The horse was the color of the Chevy Nova. Both Freddy and the Mexican were smiling. I started walking. Freddy started walking, and the closer he got to me the taller he got, until he was way up there with his head in the clouds. I pulled my revolvers, quick as the wind, as they say in Western movies, and I lifted them up and started blasting away, and Freddy leaned down from the clouds and his face came closer and closer to the ground and my bullets speckled his flesh like peppercorns, but it wasn't bothering him. He was smiling. And his eyes were as cold as the arctic wastelands. He reached out with his hands, which had become gigantic, and took me in them and began to wad me into a ball. Great gouts of blood shot out from between his fingers.

I sat up sweating. I put my back against the baseboard and wished I smoked.

The bedroom door opened. It was Russel.

"You screamed," he said.

"I did?"

"Yeah. You okay?"

"Fine. Nightmare."

"I have a lot of them."

"And after tomorrow?"

"I'll have a lot more, I guess. You sure you're okay?"

"Yeah. I'm all right."

"Well, goodnight, son," Russel said and went out.

I almost said, "Goodnight, Dad."

41.

I awoke about eleven to find Russel and Jim Bob out in the garage applying putty to the license plates of the truck. The camper and hood ornament and stripes were already on it.

"What a day I've had," I said.

"Yes sir," Jim Bob said, "worked your little fingers right down to the bone. We're gonna grab a sandwich in a minute."

"Anything I can do?"

"Not now," Russel said, and he smiled at me.

After we ate our sandwiches, Jim Bob opened a drawer in the kitchen and took out the guns he and Russel had chosen. He put them on the kitchen table and went out to the Bitch and got the sawed-off and the little ankle holster with the revolver in it. He went upstairs then and came back down with the Ithaca 12-gauge, a .45 automatic and a Western style .44. He also brought down a gun cleaning kit and several boxes of ammunition.

"Okay," Jim Bob said to me, "I'm gonna suggest you take the Ithaca. You're not used to shooting guns, and this one is very light and you can hit what you're shooting at without being a good shot. Just in case you need a backup, take one of the handguns."

I picked up the .44. Guess Ann was right, too many John Wayne movies and cowboys books. It was in a sleek, black holster, but it didn't have a belt and tie-down straps; the holster had a clip that fastened to your belt or waistband.

"Good choice," Jim Bob said. "Revolvers don't jam."

"This is a lot of artillery to kill two guys by surprise with, isn't it?" I said.

"The rules here are that there are no rules. We're gonna do it quick and fast and get out. But things can happen. As the Boy Scouts say, Be Prepared. Since we're gonna be doing this in the open, I'm gonna have us some disguises. Simple stuff. Just so we can't be recognized easy, and with the truck worked over, well, we just might get away with it. The key is to do it quick and to move on."

"We're really going to do this, aren't we?" I said.

"Damn tootin'," Jim Bob said.

After five o'clock we started over to Freddy's part of town. All three of us in the cab of the truck. Jim Bob driving, Russel in the middle, me on the passenger side. We had the revolvers and the sawed-off in a tow sack behind the seat. The sack was tied with a rope, and one end of the rope was fastened to the gun rack behind us. In the rack, in plain view, was the Ithaca. The guns had been cleaned and loaded and the glove box was full of extra ammunition, just in case we had to fight the Marines.

We got to Freddy's side of town too early because the traffic chose to be unusually moderate. We drove a few miles past Freddy's and stopped at a McDonald's for coffee. Russel hadn't said a word since we left Jim Bob's house. But he looked different. Tough again. Committed. As if during the night he had conjured up enough will to chase Old Age out of his skin. He was hard-faced, clear-eyed and level of shoulders. He looked like an old soldier about to go into battle.

At about seven-thirty, I excused myself from the McDonald's booth and went into the bathroom and threw up my coffee in the toilet. That was getting to be a habit, throwing up. If it wasn't killing somebody caused it, it was the heat or planning to kill someone. I washed my face and rinsed my mouth out by cupping water in my hand. I studied my face in the mirror. It was like after I had killed the burglar, just the same. No sign of anything on it. Just good old Richard Dane, husband and father, would-be vigilante.

I wondered if there would be much blood when we did the killing, and I wondered if they would scream. I wondered if Russel really would be able to make Freddy understand he was his father, and if it really mattered in the long run. I guess it mattered to Russel.

I rinsed my mouth again and went back and sat down next to Jim Bob and tore up my paper coffee cup, and at seven-thirty we left and headed back to Freddy's part of town.

It wasn't dark when we got there. The sky was showing gray and there was a haze of light, but the days were getting longer and they had a way of dying slowly. There was still plenty of light to see by, to shoot by, to be shot by. I felt as if we were waving a flag with Identify Us written on it.

We cruised some streets near the subdivision where Freddy lived, killing time, thinking about what we were about to do, checking our watches.

Jim Bob reached some things from under his part of the seat and tossed them into Russel's lap. "The disguises I promised."

One item was a cap with hair attached to it. The hair looked like the stuff Raggedy Ann and Andy have on top of their heads, the same carroty orange. Jim Bob took off his cowboy hat and hung it on the gun rack and reached for the cap from Russel and put it on. The orange hair hung down over his ears and almost in his eyes.

He got a pair of sunglasses off the dashboard and put them on. All he needed was a red, round nose and some floppy shoes.

Russel handed me a black wig and took a blond one for himself. There was a can of blacking there too, and Jim Bob said, "Make a mustache or something with that stuff."

Russel put on the wig and opened the can of blacking, rubbed a little on his upper lip and put a dab on his chin, passed the can to me. I put on my wig and made myself a thick mustache with the blacking, assumed I looked like Groucho Marx in a Beatle wig.

I put the blacking in the glove box and checked my watch.

Nine minutes to eight.

As we turned down the street that led to Freddy's house, Russel took hold of the rope that was attached to the bag full of guns and pulled it up.

"Careful," Jim Bob said, "them sumbitches are loaded."

"I know that, goddamnit," Russel said.

The brave assassins get jumpy. I realized I was breathing through my mouth and that I felt a touch light-headed.

Russel put the bag in his lap and opened it. He took out the sawed-off shotgun and the .38 and put them in Jim Bob's lap. Jim Bob clipped the .38's holster to his belt with one hand and held grimly to the wheel with the other. Beads of sweat were running out from under the carroty hair and down his face thick as condensation on an ice tea glass.

I took the .44 and clipped it to my belt and reached the Ithaca down from the rack and pointed the barrel at the floorboard, started counting from one hundred backwards, trying to calm myself. My hands were moist and slippery against the shotgun.

Russel had strapped Jim Bob's little ankle holster and revolver to his leg before we left the house. He had only the .357 to mess with. He put it on his knee and put one massive hand over it like a lid over a pot about to boil.

We were armed and dangerous.

We came even with Freddy's house and took a right onto a

street that led up a slight hill. We went over the hill and dipped down between a sprinkling of houses and went all the way to the end of the street and turned around slowly and started back up the hill. When we topped it and were just about to go down, the Nova showed itself. It was five minutes until eight.

Jim Bob said, "We'll go down now," and he lifted his foot to stomp the gas as the Nova started to make its careful turn into the driveway. But before Jim Bob could do what he meant to do, a green Dodge van came along behind the Nova and pulled up next to the curb just before the driveway. The Nova went on into the drive and we coasted over to the curb and stopped.

The garage door came open and the Nova coasted inside and the Mexican and Freddy got out. The driver of the van got out, went over and shook hands with the Mexican and Freddy. A man got out of the back of the van then and went over to stand in the drive and face the street, watching. We eased down in the seat and Jim Bob killed the engine. After a moment Jim Bob pulled off his cap and wig and eased his head up for a look.

"The Mex is in the house," he said. "Freddy and the other two are smoking cigarettes. The one in the drive is looking this way but he ain't acting like he sees anything. The man on the passenger side of the van is looking this way too, but he's just looking. Now he's looking to the van's front."

"Guess this is one of those unforeseen circumstances you were talking about," I said.

"That's the size of it," Jim Bob said. "The Mex is coming out and he's got some bags over his shoulders and he's carrying something. It might be a shotgun or rifle. Freddy is using the garage device, lowering the door.... No, that's not a gun the Mex has, it's a tripod. I think he's got video equipment there."

"I don't like the sound of that," Russel said.

"I should have thought that this being Friday they might have something planned for the weekend besides TV," Jim Bob said. "We should have waited until Monday."

"What's happening now?" Russel asked.

Jim Bob eased his head slightly higher. "The Mex is putting the bags and the tripod in the back of the van and the other guy that got out of the back is getting back inside. Freddy's getting in there with them. The driver is getting behind the wheel. They're turning around in the drive...heading back up the street."

We raised up.

"What do we do now?" I asked. "Wait until Monday?"

"Let's follow them a bit," Russel said. "They got in mind what I think they've got in mind, I think we should be there before they do it."

"It ain't just two fellas now," Jim Bob said. "We're talking two up front and three in the back. And that's all I saw. There might be more in the back."

"Follow them anyway," Russel said. "Hurry."

Jim Bob cranked the pickup and we went down the street briskly and made a left even more briskly. Russel and I took off our wigs and gathered them up along with Jim Bob's cap and hair and stuck them under the seat. For a killing job, they might have been all right disguises, but for tailing a car they were a little silly and obvious. Hard not to take note of Raggedy Andy, a French painter type and Groucho Marx wearing a Beatle wig.

Russel and me took turns wiping the blacking off our faces with the tow sack, wrapped the guns in it again and lowered them behind the seat. I put the Ithaca in the shotgun rack and Jim Bob put his hat on.

We saw the green van take a right onto the highway, and we gave it a few seconds before we gunned up to the intersection and went after it, managing to keep a car or two between us at all times. The van driver drove slowly and cautiously until we wound our way out of the city and out onto Highway 59 North. At that point, he picked up speed and became harder to follow. We had been after him almost an hour.

Houses fell by the wayside and great pine trees appeared in their places and shadows gathered between them like bats. There was plenty of traffic, but all that motorized activity didn't make me feel less creeped. I guess I was thinking about that young whore I had seen on the tape, or whoever she was. Just some kid, fucked and killed for Freddy's and the Mexican's entertainment.

Now we were following those selfsame murderers, as well as a number of other most likely unpleasant individuals who probably made up their steady film crew, down a dark highway with the houses and lights going away and the pines and the moon and the shadows becoming the status quo, and it was my guess that this merry little van-encased group had this night set aside for a very special little film they wished to make, and it was most certainly not a nature flick about the nocturnal mating habits of the brown moth.

We kept on going, and when we were about halfway to LaBorde, the car lights became less frequent and the night had fallen over the countryside like a hood.

We went through some little burg that consisted of a used car lot, a chicken shack, a railroad track, one red light and a fistful of abandoned buildings, and on the other side of that the van took a left and went down a narrow blacktop that seemed almost consumed by pines.

Jim Bob pulled over to the side of the road to give them a chance to get a little farther ahead so we wouldn't look so obvious. Russel got out a cigarette and lit it and I cracked my window and watched the smoke suck out it like a wraith.

"Long enough," Jim Bob said, and he checked the highway for cars and pulled across onto the blacktop. Russel leaned over me and tossed the almost whole cigarette through the crack in the window and I rolled it up. Jim Bob said, "Break out the guns."

42.

The blacktop dipped down a deep hill and wound sharply around a corner that was walled with pines, and there in the moonlight, the spears of trees on either side of it, it looked like an enormous ribbon of molasses slick enough to slide on.

We went down the hill and around the corner and down the road a piece, and no van. We went by a gravel drive and a cattle guard and finally another drive that was made of concrete, and on around another curve.

No sign of the van.

"We didn't wait that long," Jim Bob said. "They turned off."

Turning around, we went back more slowly, and as we cruised by the concrete drive, I squinted through the trees and saw lights. "There's a house down there or something," I said.

Jim Bob drove on until we came to the cattle guard, and he drove over that and parked the truck in a pasture and killed the lights.

"We can walk back and check," he said.

"And if that isn't them?" Russel asked.

"We come back to the truck and start over," Jim Bob said. "I don't think this pasture leads anywhere but more pasture, maybe

231

some trees. I think they want a house for what they're doing. The gravel drive up from this might lead to something, but let's check out the other one first."

We got out of the truck with our weapons, but didn't bother with the wigs or the blacking. Other than those we intended to eliminate, witnesses out here were few and far between. And we didn't need the blacking to protect us from being exposed in the moonlight. The moon was just a sliver and the shadows were thick and would conceal us as well as anything might.

The air had cooled off with nightfall, but I was having trouble breathing it; it felt too heavy and thick to go through my nose and mouth.

Jim Bob led and Russel and I followed. Just before we came to the drive, Jim Bob said, "If it's them, take it easy. We'll see what we got and put together some kind of game plan. When it comes down to assholes and elbows, remember this: We're outnumbered, but we can surprise them. That element doesn't go as far in real life as it does in the movies, but it's something. When this shindig gets started, don't shoot to wing anybody. This is the once and for all real thing, and when the smoke clears, we want to be standing, or at least breathing."

"Remember," Russel said, "you're going to try and leave Freddy for me."

"Me and Dane ain't gonna get killed so you can get your shot in, but if it's within our power he's yours."

Car lights curved around the road and we darted into the high grass and peeked out. It was the gray Vette.

"The guy from the video store," I said.

We watched the taillights go brighter as it slowed, turned onto the concrete drive.

"I think we found our boys," Jim Bob said.

When we reached the driveway, we stopped short of that and took to the right of it and moved through some brush and scrub trees. The closer we came to the house, the clearer the terrain became, and we finally came to a spot where the brush ended and there was a row of briars like concentration camp barbed wire, and beyond that a scattering of tall pines. Off to the far right, the land and brush tumbled into a ravine. On the other side of the drive it was the same way with the brush ending and the cleared land and the scattered trees taking over, only there was no ravine on that side. Artfully arranged at the end of the drive between the pines was a tall house of glass and redwood and there were lights on in the house and we could see stairs with a man on them, and walking behind him was Freddy. I recognized him by his bulk and the way he moved—like his old man. The stairs turned at the top and went behind a wall and they were soon out of sight.

Outside the house there were several men standing around, five to be exact, and the thin man in the white suit got out of the Vette and a girl got out on the other side and they went over to join them. I couldn't tell much about the girl, but she didn't seem to be forced. But that didn't mean anything. She wouldn't have been told the entire plan—the shooting part would have been left out. She was short and had long, black hair to her waist and she walked with plenty of hip roll and had nice hips for the rolling.

One of the men in the group said loudly, "You pull train, baby?" The guy in the white suit said, "Speak Mex," and the man spoke again in that language, the same question I presume, because the girl laughed musically and her *Sí* drifted back to us and was followed by male laughter sharp and desperate as the barking of caged dogs.

Everyone, except a man who looked like a boulder in a suit, went in the house. The boulder took up a position by the door and folded his hands in front of him and cupped his crotch like he was weighing his testicles.

"Think she's a pigeon?" Russel said.

"Probably," Jim Bob said. "I think we're going to have to play it that way. But watch for her. She could be with them and have a gun and she just might shoot your dick off. You two go toward the house by the ravine, and I'm gonna cross the drive when I get the chance and come up on the other side. I'm good at this sneaking stuff."

"Hear you tell it," Russel said, "there isn't anything you aren't good at."

"I don't whistle too well," Jim Bob said. "Now remember, we've seen six guys outside, two going up the stairs. That makes eight. But there might be more inside. And don't forget the girl. Like I said, she may not be friendly."

"We'll do this simple, come up on both sides of the fella at the door, and whoever gets there first takes him out. I won't wait on you, and you don't wait on me. And the thing then is to get started, to go on in the house and start shooting any one of those sonofabitches that you see. When you get inside, move like you mean it. Seek and shoot, upstairs and downstairs. Keep count of how many you drop, and get the killing in your blood. Get goddamn good and self-righteous about it because that's the only way you'll see it through."

"Merciful Jesus," I said.

"It's a pisser, ain't it?" Jim Bob said. "Now, y'all get started."

Russel and I eased down into the ravine by sliding on the slick grass and dry clay that made up the sides. Our feet landed in a thin trickle of brackish-smelling water and sent up a cloud of mosquitoes that lit on our faces, hands, backs, and shoulders and sucked blood even through our shirts. Roots and brush tumbled and twisted across the floor of the ravine, grabbed at our feet and tried to trip us. Above us, jutting out from the lips of the ravine, arthritic trees and scrubby brush hid a lot of the thin moonlight and made our path down there damn dark. Still, we stepped quickly, and quietly. At least, I hoped we were moving quietly. I couldn't hear all that well on account of my blood pounding in my temples.

The scrub brush and trees diminished above us and the light from the house was stronger than the bad moonlight and it fell down into the ravine like tainted butter. The ravine went narrow and the left side of it dropped down and we had to bend low and ease over to the edge of it and poke our heads up to see exactly where we were.

We were almost even with the front edge of the house, and I could see the boulder in the suit standing under a yellow bug light on the front porch. I wondered about him; couldn't help but think he might be thinking about what was going on inside the house and wishing he was in on it, but was stuck instead with guard duty. And maybe he wasn't thinking about it at all, didn't care. Perhaps he was thinking about fast cars and women and the Dallas Cowboys, the price of special made suits that would fit his boulder-shaped body.

I looked at Russel.

"Let's take him," he whispered.

43.

"I've got the shotgun," I said. "I guess I should do it."

Russel didn't try to talk me out of it. I waited a second or two hoping he would, then went over the lip of the ravine with a shell pumped into the chamber and before I was halfway there the guy torqued and saw me and reached inside his coat. I was about to fire at him, when Jim Bob, like some kind of cowboy-hatted ghost, swooped out of the night and hit the man in the side of the head with the barrel of the sawed-off. The man spun almost around and Jim Bob kicked his feet out from under him. The man's head hit the concrete porch with a soft smack and Jim Bob bent over him, made a quick move with his hand and stood up.

All in all, the entire undertaking had been relatively quiet.

I came up alongside Jim Bob, then Russel moved up behind me, breathing sharply. I looked down at the man on the ground. Jim Bob's sawed-off was lying across his chest and underneath the man's chin was a swathe of darkness; as I watched, it grew broader. Jim Bob had a pocketknife in his hand and the blade was dripping blood. He closed it on his pants leg, pushed it into his pants pocket and picked up the sawed-off. "It's Howdy Doody time," he said and jerked the door open and went inside, Russel and I behind him. No one was there for us to shoot at.

Jim Bob nodded up the stairs, and went that way. Russel went right and I went left, the shotgun in front of me. I came to a door and opened it and found a closet. None of the coats tried to get me. I closed the door and went around the corner and down the hall, and then the world started rocking and rolling with the sound of gunfire. It was coming from upstairs. I started to turn, then heard running feet. I whirled and crouched, and one of the men from the van came beating toward me. When he saw me, he tried to slow down, and it was like one of those comic takes, where the comedian does a kind of choppy half-step, half-skid backwards. But this guy wasn't a comedian. His hand went inside his coat and it came out with a revolver and I cut down on him with the Ithaca and took him full in the chest. He spun and went down, but rolled on his back and got to a near-sitting position and took a shot at me; the bullet burned along my neck. I pumped another load into the Ithaca and fired again and caught the guy in the chin and the shot made his head cock way too far back and he flopped on the floor and the hall filled with the odor of shit and gunpowder.

Shooting had been going on all the while, and I decided to go on down the hall and see what was there, then go back to the stairs and hope for the best. I jumped over the dead man and went around the corner expecting gunfire, but finding only a big empty kitchen with the makings of a sandwich on the counter. The guy must have been fixing himself a snack when the shooting started. I ran back up the hall and took a left toward the stairway, saw a blur of movement, dropped to one knee, and pumped a load into the Ithaca as I did. A man with one arm dangling limp and awkward at his side, an automatic hanging from one finger like a knickknack on a hook, stumbled backwards and fell against one of the big windowpanes that made up the front of the house, and began to slide down it, leaving a road of blood on the glass. Russel came into view, walked over to the man, put the .357 to the top of his head and shot him.

"Russel," I said.

He wheeled on me and the revolver cocked, then lifted up. His eyes were stoned looking and his face was as white as a Ku Kluxer's sheet.

"Stairs," he said.

There was gunfire up there, and when we got to the turn in the stairway, we found a Mexican. Not the one we were familiar with, but another. The top of his head was gone.

We went over him, on up fast, then a door came open at the top of the stairs and there was a scream like a dinosaur in pain, and Jim Bob came flying out, smashed against the wall and melted onto the landing. He had lost his hat and like Russel his eyes were wild looking and his face was dead white. He still had the sawed-off in his hand. The .38 was gone from its holster.

It wasn't Jim Bob screaming. It was the one Jim Bob called the Mex. He stumbled out of the doorway and onto the landing. The front of his shirt was dark and wet and the material sucked into his chest when he breathed. He looked as if he were wired up on something.

Jim Bob rolled his head toward us. "Shoot the motherfucker," he yelled. "I gave him both barrels."

Russel's .357 rode up and bucked and the Mex's head snapped hard right and back around as if on a spring. Half his face was gone. The Mex reached down and grabbed Jim Bob by the leg and slung him at us. Jim Bob hit me and I went back, fell over the dead Mexican on the stairs. Russel was still where he was.

The Mex was coming down the steps after Russel like the Frankenstein monster. Russel lifted his gun hand and used his other hand to brace his wrist and he shot the Mex in the nose and the Mex doubled forward and tumbled down over Jim Bob and me and the other Mexican.

Russel continued up the stairs. Jim Bob got to his feet, broke open the sawed-off, and got two shells out of his snap shirt pocket and loaded the gun and flicked it shut.

I got hold of the Ithaca, which I had momentarily lost, and I went up after Jim Bob. Russel went through the door just ahead of us, and we rushed in after him.

The room was the room where they had made the video we had seen. A video camera was on a tripod at the far right, and another lay overturned on the floor. A third without a tripod lay on the corner of the bed. A man lay on the bed too. It was the man I had seen going up the stairs ahead of Freddy; I recognized his suit. He was lying on top of the girl. I couldn't tell anything about her. I could only see the bottom of her naked feet, her arms thrown out as if in crucifixion, and her black hair spread against the white sheets like an oil spill on snow.

"Freddy and that skinny fuck are around here somewhere," Jim Bob said. "Them and this guy and the Mex were in here when I came in. The skinny guy was putting the meat to her."

I went over to the man on the bed and grabbed him by the collar of his suit and pulled him off the girl. He rolled face up. He looked like a man that had never had to work. He had very fine silver hair and a matching mustache. He must have been fifty at least. Old enough to have been the girl's father. Jim Bob had shot him several times in the chest and crotch. With the .38 most likely. The wounds were small.

I looked at the girl. She didn't move anything but her eyes. They rolled toward me. They were the color of old pecans. The nipples of her small breasts were uncommonly large and wide and matched the color of her eyes. Her pubic hair was so neatly trimmed it looked like little fur panties. Her short legs were shiny, as if oiled. I figured her for about eighteen. Under the circumstances, she was about as sexy as an avocado. I could see now that there were thin, white cords tied to her wrists and in turn to the bedpost. I didn't try to untie them. No time for that. I gave her what I thought was a reassuring smile. If she caught the meaning, her face and eyes gave no sign of it. She just lay there quietly, watching, perhaps resigned.

There was just the one door on the far left, where Russel was, and a closet door between the bed and that exit. Jim Bob cocked the triggers on the sawed-off, jerked the closet door open, and the skinny guy, buck naked, came out of there with a scream and a flash of knife and the blade went down and over Jim Bob's shoulder and poked him deep in the back. Jim Bob hit the man in the stomach with both barrels of the shotgun and pulled the triggers. Red jumped out of the skinny guy, front and back, and he flopped to the floor. Jim Bob went to his knees and bent his head. The knife stuck out of his back like a quill.

Russel, without hardly looking, reached over and took it by the handle and pulled it out with a jerk.

"Goddamn!" Jim Bob said.

Russel stuck the knife through his belt and opened the door in front of him and stepped quickly to the side, but nobody fired at him.

"Freddy," Russel yelled into the room. "I'm Ben Russel. I'm your father. I've come to kill you."

I went around behind Russel and peeked through the doorway and Russel moved inside and I followed. Jim Bob got up, leaned against the door jamb and said, "That hurt, Ben."

The room was a big office room and there was a metal desk and chair and file cabinets against the wall and a big freestanding fireplace. I saw part of a pants leg behind the fireplace, then part of a shoulder and a face. Freddy.

I jerked up the Ithaca, but a hand came down on top of the barrel and the gun fired into the floor. It was Jim Bob. "There he is, Ben, the fireplace," Jim Bob said.

Freddy stepped out from behind it and lifted a pistol and shot Jim Bob, sent him sprawling backwards. He fired again and hit Jim Bob a second time and knocked him through the open doorway.

"I'm your father," Russel said, and the .357 came up, but not fast enough. Freddy shot Russel in the right shoulder and the shot knocked the gun out of his hand. Russel went to one knee with a grunt.

I brought the shotgun around again, and fired. The shot knocked the hell out of the freestanding fireplace and a section of it came off and hit the floor and the fireplace wasn't freestanding anymore. But I didn't hit Freddy.

Freddy shot at me as I pumped another load into the Ithaca, and the shot punched a hole in my side and my right arm went numb and the shotgun swung wide right as if on a gate and went to the floor. I tried to reach for the .44 in the holster by cross drawing with my left hand, but knew damn well I'd never make it. I was looking down the barrel of Freddy's gun, the mouth of death about to spit in my eye.

Russel's ankle gun barked, and Freddy let out his air as if punched. He sat down on the floor and his gun fell between his legs. "Shit, I'm shot," he said.

He looked at the gun on the floor in front of him and reached out to get it, but his fingers wouldn't cooperate and take hold. It was as if they were trying to clutch mercury. He quit trying. He just sat there looking at the gun as if it had betrayed him. He coughed and a ball of blood spotted his chin.

Russel walked over to him. He had the little ankle gun in his left hand and his right arm was folded in front of him out of my sight.

"I didn't want it to hurt," Russel said. "I wanted it done clean because I love you."

Freddy smiled and looked up. "Love me? Man, you just put a hole in me. Shit, you really my daddy?"

"Uh huh," Russel said.

"If that isn't some kind of trip," Freddy said, and Russel shot him through the forehead.

44.

The numbness had mostly gone out of my side, though my arm, for some reason I couldn't fathom, felt like a wet Kleenex. I reached across with my left hand and felt where the bullet had gone in and out through my shirt and flesh, but neither wound seemed particularly dreadful. I didn't seem to be bleeding much. I let that give me some comfort.

I left Russel standing over his dead son, went in and knelt down by Jim Bob. The trip from one room to the other assured me all my parts were working, and more feeling was coming back into my arm; it felt like it had gone to sleep and was struggling to wake up.

Russel came in and got down on his knees by me and reached out and touched Jim Bob's arm. Jim Bob opened his eyes and looked at us.

"I thought you weren't going to do that," Russel said.

"It seemed like the right thing at the time," Jim Bob said. "I don't think I'd do it again, though."

"Bad?" Russel said.

"Bad enough that Rodriguez is going to make some money. You look a mite peaked yourself."

"A mite," Russel said.

"Dane?"

"I'm hit," I said. "I feel okay though. I think it went through the fat meat on the side. I'm not even bleeding much."

"You got a cut on your neck," Jim Bob said.

I reached up and touched where a bullet had sliced me, came away with blood on my hand. "They seem to be shooting all around the edges," I said.

Russel touched Jim Bob's forehead. "No fever," he said.

"I haven't got the flu," Jim Bob said. "God, did we get them all?"

"Uh huh," Russel said.

"Damn, we're better than I thought," Jim Bob said.

"Can you get the truck?" Russel asked me. "I must be getting old. I feel winded." His eyes were full of tears.

"Yeah," I said.

"The girl seemed all right didn't she?" Jim Bob said.

I glanced over at the bed. She hadn't gone anywhere. Her face was turned toward us, those pecan-colored eyes taking us in.

"She's okay," I said. "Just scared shitless."

I got the keys out of Jim Bob's pocket and walked to the truck and drove it back. Upstairs, Russel had used the skinny man's knife to cut off the side of the sheet the girl was lying on (I bet she enjoyed seeing him coming toward her with that wicked knife), and had used it to make bandages for Jim Bob. When I got there, Russel took off his shirt and I used some of the sheet to bandage him, then he did the same for me. We put our shirts on, and I went looking for our guns, including Jim Bob's lost .38 which he said the Mexican had swatted from him and knocked across the room. I found it twisted in the thin man's white suit, which lay on the floor beside the bed.

I put all the guns in the truck, then Russel and I used our good arms to carry Jim Bob downstairs and over the dead bodies. We dropped him only once. He cussed until the air sizzled. We put him in the camper and gave him his hat to lay on his chest, then

Russel and I went upstairs and cut the girl loose, found her clothes under the bed, and turned our backs while she put them on. When she was dressed, we led her downstairs. She didn't say so much as one word and her eyes told me she still hadn't figured us out. After what she'd been through, she was entitled to doubt and silence.

We put her in the back of the truck with Jim Bob and Russel climbed in there too and rested his back against the cab and found one of his cigarettes and lit it and coughed some smoke out.

"You sure you can drive?" he asked me.

"I'm not seeing spots or anything," I said. "My side hurts, but my left hand is good. My right hand has more feeling than it had just a few minutes ago."

"Get weak, we'll swap on the driving," Russel said.

"I'll go as fast as I can without bringing the law down on us," I said. "I'll try not to make it too rough a ride, Jim Bob."

"Don't pamper me," Jim Bob said. "I ain't gonna die or nothing. Long as they didn't shoot my dick off, I'm gonna be okay."

I closed the back of the camper and went around and got behind the wheel and drove us away from that big house full of death.

45.

It was a hot Sunday afternoon in August and I was sitting at the picnic table out back of the house drinking a cold Lone Star, alternating between watching the condensation beads on the beer bottle and my son playing on his new swing set.

I had been sitting there thinking about my family. About the things I had done. The hands that had hugged my son earlier were the same hands that had held guns that had been used to kill people. It didn't seem right somehow. Even though the day was bright, when I thought about these things, I had the sensation of shadows moving behind my eyes. Perhaps they were the sort of shadows Russel had waltzed with, and now I had dancing partners of my own. And Russel had enough for hell's own minuet.

It had been almost a month since the shoot-out, and not a day, a waking moment, had gone by without me thinking about it. It had replaced my thoughts about the burglar I had shot, and even the soft, little face of the daughter I had never known. The memory of that night was so strong I could sometimes smell the gun smoke, blood, and fear. The experience had been exhilarating, like driving a car too fast, walking a high wire without a net. Better than either of those things could be. After those intense few moments of blood and thunder, I found myself wanting to do it again. Life now seemed remarkably tame and fearfully constant.

And when the desire to recall or repeat those moments of fire and steel passed, I would fill up with a cold self-hatred and a longing for my soul. Not in a religious sense. I couldn't believe there was anything on the other side of the void, not after what I had seen. But in the personal sense. I feared my humanity was threatening to ooze out of me, perhaps through a hole in the bottom like Russel had described.

My side and neck had healed nicely with only minor scarring, thanks to Rodriguez, and James and Valerie had been handling things at work quite well, during what I called my sabbatical.

I had gotten a card from Jim Bob saying he and Russel were "right as rain," and I had read several newspaper accounts of the shoot-out. The Dixie Mafia was getting most of the blame. But Freddy Russel turning up again, dead for real this time, had proved most-embarrassing to the FBI. Especially since the local cop who identified the body through mug shots and the like had turned this information over to the newspapers who grabbed it like a football and ran with it as far as they thought it would go, and that proved to be pretty far.

The papers also identified the silver-haired man. He was a rich industrialist and his house was found to be full of snuff films. Some in which he starred and personally delivered the *coup de grâce*. There was lots of speculation about the whole thing, but none of it seemed to be leading to us, so I quit worrying.

Anyway, I was out back drinking my beer, thinking about all this, and Ann came out and said, "That man is here to see you," and from the way she looked and spoke, I knew who it was immediately.

"I want him away from here," she said. "Once is enough. I won't have you going off with him again, for anything. Not even a Coke. Don't offer him anything."

"All right," I said. Ann hadn't forgiven Russel for Jordan, and even though I had never been able to explain to her the whole of the night at the house, she had a good enough idea what went on there without me giving it to her in painterly detail, and she blamed him for that too.

She called Jordan in with a promise of milk and cookies, and he bailed out of the swing and ran by me and grabbed my leg. I picked him up and held him in front of me. "Love you, Daddy," he said.

"I love you too," I said, and holding him was like touching some source of power. The emptiness I feared went away and I was filled again. For a time. I kissed him and put him down and patted him on the butt. He ran in after his mama, and I went on through the living room and outside.

Russel was in the drive leaning on Rodriguez's Rambler. I walked over and shook his hand, but was easy about it. From the way he held it out I could tell his arm still hurt.

"I was trying to decide if I should come by or not," he said. "I didn't want to upset Ann. I saw her looking at me through the window, and I figured she'd go get you. I shouldn't have come, I guess."

"I wanted to see you," I said.

"I see the bars on your windows are gone."

"I felt like a canary. I got rid of them."

"Good. Jim Bob said to tell you the burglar's name was William Randolph. Mean anything?"

I shook my head. "I had forgotten about that, to tell you the truth. How'd he find out?"

"You'll like this. He called Price, said he read in the papers about Freddy Russel, and since that was Freddy Russel, the guy you shot couldn't have been him, and he figured Price owed you something after sicking those thugs with the bats on us."

I laughed. "That sounds like Jim Bob."

"Price didn't even argue. He gave Jim Bob the name. He probably figures we were in on the action at that house, one way or another, but I don't think he cares. I think he's glad it's over, and he's probably glad the scum bit the dust. It's not his job to help the FBI protect anyone anymore."

"How is Jim Bob?" I asked.

"Good. Nothing bothers him long. He might even be the super-man he thinks he is. The Mexican girl we got out of the house is taking care of him. He's already getting around pretty good. He's going to send the girl home to Mexico next week, give her a little nest egg to take with her."

"That sounds like him," I said. "What are you going to do now?"

"Nothing left to do. A man that can kill his own son, no matter what he's done, is bankrupt of something. Soul. What have you. I put his photographs with that foul tape and burned them up, tried to burn up anything I might have felt about him. But I couldn't. You know, I still love him after all he's done, and I never really knew him. This won't mean much, Richard. But if I could have had the kind of son I wanted, I would have wanted him to be exactly like you."

"It means a lot."

"I only wish I hadn't gotten you involved in this mess."

"You couldn't have stopped me."

He took me then and hugged me, and I hugged him back. It made me think of the last time I saw my father, before he went away and put the gun in his mouth.

When we pulled apart, Russel said, "That's all I got in me."

I was trembling slightly. It was hard to speak.

He walked around and got in the car and rolled down the window. "I got this for Jordan." He reached a red toy fire truck off the seat and gave it to me. "You don't have to tell him it isn't from you. Maybe when he gets older, if he remembers that night...well, you can tell him...just tell him, okay?"

"Yeah."

"Keep the shadows away, Richard."

"I'll do my best, Ben."

He backed the Rambler around and rolled down the drive and I waved at the retreating car, not knowing if he could see me in the rearview mirror or not. I turned and started back to the house. There was a loud report. It made my blood surge and I felt the exhilaration I had felt that night of the shooting. I whirled, realized immediately that the old Rambler had backfired. The rush went away. I felt scared then, because for a moment, the sound, so like a gunshot, had flooded me with a tide of clear, clean joy. And now that the tide was gone, I was disappointed. That's what frightened me. The disappointment.

"No shadows," I said aloud, and as I walked through the front door, I repeated it like a charm against evil. "No shadows."

AFTERWORD

Once Again, It's *Cold in July*

Joe R. Lansdale

My usual method of working is that I feel a kind of mental nudge that indicates a story is lying in wait in my subconscious, and I should be alert that it is trying to speak to me. Then, a little later, the opening or the basic idea will widen and present itself.

Once that happens, each day I get up ready to go, and the story, as if hidden behind a door, waits until my usual work time (morning), opens, and I pass into another room where the story is given to me a piece at the time. You see, for me, a story generally has many rooms. This moving to new rooms and opening new doors happens every morning until the story is finished. That's a lot of doors. A lot of rooms.

At least, that's how it usually is.

Now and again it works differently, and a novel (more frequently, a short story) will jump full-blown into my consciousness. It's an amazing thing. As if the gods have leaned down and said, "Here, take this. I love you today. And you know what, you look good. You working out?"

No novel has ever come to me more full-blown than *Cold in*

July. I can pinpoint the moment the idea was driven into my head like a nail.

My wife and I decided perhaps it would be best if we bought a new house. We had a four-year-old son, Keith, and a baby daughter, Kasey, and things in our house were becoming tight, especially where my work space was concerned. Kasey had taken over my study, transforming it into a baby room. The crib was tucked in there amidst file cabinets, shelves, and stacks of books. My work desk was covered with diapers and baby supplies.

I turned to writing on a small desk in our bedroom. It wobbled. I folded cardboard and placed it under the bad leg to balance it out. Still it wobbled when I typed, and I had to be alert enough to catch the typewriter if it began to slide toward the edge, which it did with gradual certainty as I worked. When I typed, I really went at it. I was using an electric typewriter then, and at the time I was wearing one out nearly every year. They were Montgomery Ward typewriters, and they still had keys, not a rotating ball like an IBM. I pounded so hard on those machines sometimes the keys flew off.

A number of my books were written with daily interruptions to take care of the children while my wife worked as a fire department dispatcher. On the days when she was home, I doubled up on my work schedule. This was long before I came to work three hours a day in the mornings. Back then, I worked every chance I had, not knowing when the kids would need attention, not only to be fed, diapers changed, and the like, but time spent with them in play. Family first, but since the family also needed to eat, I gave that machine regular exercise.

As our home was being transformed by our children, I was about to start my novel *The Drive-In*, and we had a little money for a change, so we decided we were ready to buy a new home, something that better fit our growing family.

We saw several houses over the next few weeks and found one that was promising, out by the lake. It looked right and we were very interested, but when we walked into the living room, I happened to look up, and there in the ceiling was most certainly a bullet hole.

According to the realtor, there were no stories of gunfights or murder, and the hole was probably due to a gun accident. I had two thoughts immediately: some domestic argument where one of those involved fired a dramatic shot into the ceiling, or as the realtor suggested, a careless accident. I never did find out the truth.

I don't know if that bullet hole put us off the house, but something about it didn't appeal in the long run, so we delayed our house shopping for a while. But that night, after seeing that house, back home I kept thinking about that damn bullet hole. I knew there was a story there, and if I didn't know the true one, my mind wanted to invent one.

When it was bedtime, I fell fast asleep and then awoke in the middle of the night having discovered, at least story-wise, that I knew exactly why that bullet hole was there. I had dreamed the opening of a novel. It was intense, seemed to be about me and my family. Therefore, it was more than a little disturbing. I went to the bathroom, and washed my face, and returned to bed, thinking I had something to work with for a book, I'd just have to figure it from there, but a few hours later, I woke up with a larger chunk of the novel in mind. I repeated the face washing, went back to sleep, repeated this rising and face washing all night, and by morning, the entire novel was in my head and my face was very clean. I was also tired.

Frankly, I didn't know if it was worth writing right then. It was so rare for a novel to be so logical and straightforward when based on dreams, I was suspicious. I often use dreams for short stories, sometimes as is, but novels are generally more cut and paste from dreams, meaning only bits and pieces work for inspiration, and I have to wipe it all down smooth with logic. This one, it seemed, was laid out, step by step, including the personalities of side characters like Jim Bob Luke and Lt. Price.

As fate would have it, one of the events that had given us a financial leg up was a nonfiction anthology of Western facts and legend. It was supposed to come out from Bantam books. My editor, Greg Tobin, came to East Texas from New Jersey, where he lived, to visit and edit the anthology. While he was there, one day as we sat at the kitchen table about to eat lunch, my wife strategically said, "Joe, tell Greg your dream."

I did.

He liked it.

He said if I would type up a synopsis and send it to him, he would buy it.

It wasn't until that moment that I actually knew I had a novel.

Oddly, the nonfiction book Greg came to work on never appeared from Bantam. Something changed and they decided to cut their losses before it came out. I got paid, but the book, with a co-editor, appeared from another publisher years later as two coffee-table books.

I disliked telling a novel idea to anyone, as that takes the heat off a story for me. I'm pretty mum when I'm working on a project, but this one was so clear and so laid out, it didn't dilute my energy on the project at all. I had not only told my wife the story in detail, I had now told an editor, and he was interested. It's the one and only time, after becoming a professional, where I actually talked a story out to someone, including my wife. I think I did it well, but I was afraid telling it would suck the juice from it. I had that happen before, and because of that had learned not to run my mouth. But again, this felt different. It was as if it had already been written and all I had to do was find the completed pages. The only thing I had to add later was the job my character had, and a name for the town where he lived. In my dream, he kept going to some office or another, and that was never clearly defined. I decided I wanted something very solid and simple. My friend Bob LaBorde owned a frame shop, and I borrowed his profession for my main character and narrator, and used Bob's last name as the name for the town. He gets an acknowledgment in the book.

I also did a bit of research with the police department about certain things, and as I was acquainted with a number of police officers, the answers to these questions were only a phone call away.

I was ready to go, except I had to write a novel I called *The Drive-In*, as it was due first, so I wrote it rapidly. Oddly, it too was a dream, but unlike *Cold in July*, which seemed very logical and straightforward, *The Drive-In* required a lot of cutting and pasting and mind-numbing work to make it seem both surreal and real at the same time. Like most of my work, with *The Drive-In*, I had no idea where it would go from day to day. That said, and for all the mental grief it gave me, it came rapidly.

As a side note, at the time, I thought *The Drive-In* was the world's biggest loser and was worried about it. When I turned it in to Pat LoBrutto, my editor at Doubleday (soon to be part of the same company that owned Bantam), he loved it. I didn't know that right away, and while I was waiting for Pat to read it, I took a breath, and pretty much, right on the back of *The Drive-In*, started *Cold in July*.

I wrote a few pages of *Cold in July*, which I was itching to write, and it didn't feel right. I was confident I had the story, but not about the method of telling it. I started worrying about the background of all the characters. I happened to call my friend Ardath Mayhar that day, admitting to her I wasn't entirely satisfied with what I had done, that it didn't ring true, and that really bothered me. I feared that maybe I had talked out the story after all.

Immediately she said, "What person is it in?"

"Third," I said.

"Change it to first. That's what made *The Magic Wagon* so good."

I had just finished *The Drive-In*, which is written in first person, so maybe that's why I hesitated originally, I don't know, but when she said that, I knew she was right. I changed it.

And like *The Drive-In*, it leaped from my typewriter, but unlike

The Drive-In, I felt it was good from the first page. It seemed clearer to me, as the plot was already laid out in my head, and I was greatly enjoying writing a crime story. My first novel was a crime story, and crime had been an element of other things I had written, but I wanted this one to be a tribute to Gold Medal books, to John D. McDonald specifically.

It ran like a deer all the way through, and when I looked up about two and a half months later, it was finished.

It was published shortly after *The Drive-In*, and both of those books got a lot of attention and turned my career around. *Cold in July* was optioned pretty soon after its appearance by director John Irvin. He had it for seven years, and I wrote several versions of the screenplay, and finally I thought the screenplay had been altered too much, and threw in the towel. So did John.

The novel lay fallow for years, popped in and out of print, had a few film bites here and there, but nothing that interested me. And then along came film director Jim Mickle and screenwriter and actor Nick Damici. They wanted to option it. They wanted to make a film. A screenplay was written, and I loved it. Over the years, it was revised a few times, but mostly got better, and toward the end was very good. They kept renewing the option. We all stuck together, and finally one day I got the news it was actually being made. There was no cast, but there was financing.

The shooting schedule was tight, and they pretty much had to start right away. Problem was, there was no cast. But the actors seemed to fall out of the sky. Not any actors—the right actors. When I heard Michael C. Hall was going to be the lead, I thought, of course, he's perfect. I didn't know it until I heard it, but I knew it when I did. Same with Sam Shepard, and if anyone personified my character Jim Bob Luke, it's Don Johnson. Vinessa Shaw was also perfect as Ann, and Wyatt Russell...well, see the film. He's good. And on top of all that, it was being shot in period, 1989, when the novel appeared.

Sweet.

My wife and I had already arranged to spend six weeks in Italy before we knew the shooting schedule, and as it turned out, the first week of shooting began the last week we were there. I love Italy, one of my favorite places in the world, but enjoyable a time as we were having, that first week of shooting I was really wired to come home and see what was shaking as far as the film was concerned. Jim gave me updates by e-mail, but I wanted to be there.

We finished our Italian trip, flew back to the States, decompressed at home for a couple of days, and then my whole family flew out to the site. We were fortunate enough to spend two weeks on the set. I had been on film sets before, but this was an amazing experience. From the first moment I was there, I knew my book was in good hands. Everyone involved—the director, the actors, the crew, the producers, and the stunt people, whom I adored— were so focused, and sincere, and fun-loving, it couldn't have been otherwise.

Cold in July was coming to life.

We were off to the races.

Since its first appearance, *Cold in July* has been in a number of editions, here and foreign, but for some odd reason in the U.S., in the last few years it has lain fallow, except for a relatively recent e-book version. I missed a paper copy not being available, but now there is this new edition with an introduction by Jim Mickle and an afterword by me. That makes me happy. Over the years, it's been called a cult favorite, a classic, a reader's favorite, what have you. I don't know about that. I hope it's true. But I do know this: it's nice to see a book you always felt deserved extended attention receiving just that, boosted by a film based on it.

I hope you enjoy reading it as much as I enjoyed writing it. It was one of my finest experiences as a writer. Having a story so solid and powerful waiting in the wings, sitting down to write it, and having it fall out of my head directly into the typewriter, my tool of trade at that time, was highly satisfying.

Enough.

I wrote the book, and now it's yours, for a small fee.

Read away.

And if you read at night, I hope it makes you want to keep the lights on.